THE BRIDAL
BARGAIN

… the resignation letter she had been working on for the last three hours. Now it was … and there was nothing to stop her from … it off and posting it, but somehow she … bring herself to do so—not yet.

… got up and paced the floor, and then on … sudden impulse she picked up her keys and … for the door.

It was a beautiful, warm summer's day and … gardens of the cottages that lined her path … the village street overflowed with flowers, … an idyllic scene.

… Normally just the sight of them would have … enough to lift her spirits and make her … how fortunate she was to live where she … and be the person she was, a person with … a job she loved, a family she loved, a life … loved.

… but not a man she loved … The man she … And not the job she loved either— … for, though the school and her work … important to her, they did not come any …

THE BRIDAL BARGAIN

BY

EMMA DARCY

MILLS & BOON®

First published in Great Britain 2002
Large Print edition 2002
Harlequin Mills & Boon Limited,
Eton House, 18-24 Paradise Road,
Richmond, Surrey TW9 1SR

© Emma Darcy 2002

ISBN 0 263 17368 2

Set in Times Roman 17 on 19 pt.
16-1102-41801

Printed and bound in Great Britain
by Antony Rowe Ltd, Chippenham, Wiltshire

CHAPTER ONE

JOB day!

Hannah O'Neill rolled out of her bunk in the youth hostel, collected the necessities and raced for the shower block, needing an early start this morning. She had to prime herself up for the interview which would win her the job she wanted. Of course, there were probably other jobs she could get, and certainly her financial situation demanded that she snag one this week, but chef on board a luxury catamaran doing day-trips to The Great Barrier Reef was definitely a plum position.

It was to be hoped that whoever was doing the hiring had been so impressed by her brilliant résumé of previous experience, they hadn't checked every minute detail. Not that she'd actually lied. Kitchen hands did assist chefs so saying she'd been an assistant chef was a perfectly reasonable statement. And a take-away fish and fries shop was a seafood restaurant—more or less.

All she needed was the chance to talk her way into being given the opportunity to prove she was as good as her word. It was her one great talent—convincing people she could do anything. Lots of zippy energy and confidence—that was all it took. Plus being a nice person to have around; cheerful disposition, ample tolerance, ready smile, never too proud to appeal for help.

On her two-year journey of discovery around Australia, these well-developed qualities had won her work whenever she had needed to replenish her bank balance. There was only the east coast left to explore now. She'd come across The Top End to Cooktown and down the Bloomfield Track to Cape Tribulation. Next stop, Port Douglas, where she hoped to stay for the main tourist season— May to November—provided she got a job.

The job, if luck was with her.

As she showered and washed her hair, Hannah gave herself the pleasure of remembering the wonderful days she'd had here at Cape Tribulation; hiking through the fantastic Daintree Forest which was as primeval in its own way as the ancient Kimberley Outback, then the incredible contrast of Myall Beach, surely the most beautiful beach in the world with its brilliant white sand and turquoise water.

It was sad to be leaving, but needs must, she told herself. Her shoestring budget was running out of string. Besides, Port Douglas and The Great Barrier Reef would undoubtedly prove a great new adventure. And it was time to get in touch with her family again to let them know she was still alive. Not that they worried overmuch about her. All the O'Neills had been brought up to be resourceful. But it was always nice to call in and catch up on the family gossip.

It would be interesting to find out if the faithless Flynn was still happily married to her ex-best friend, for whom he'd virtually jilted Hannah at the altar. Two years on…the honeymoon period would definitely be over by now. Some darkly malevolent thoughts skated through Hannah's mind. It was easy to say forgive and forget, move on. She'd certainly moved on, and on, and on, but forgiving and forgetting…not easy at all!

Nevertheless, today was a day for looking ahead and that was what she was going to do. The past was gone. No changing the Flynn-and-Jodie blot on the landscape of her life but it was a long way behind her now and she'd enjoyed a lot of bright and shiny days, weeks, months, since then. And if she got the job on *Duchess,* that would be as good as being a duchess.

Having towelled herself dry, she pulled on her clean jeans and the stretchy, no-wrinkle midriff top striped in green and blue and black and lipstick pink. It was a brilliant little top. Not only did it go with everything she carried with her, it showed off the great tan she'd acquired and picked up the green in her eyes.

Her long, crinkly blonde hair always took ages to dry, but the road trip to Port Douglas would probably consume the whole morning. She would have plenty of time to put it into a neat plait before the interview, which wasn't until three o'clock this afternoon. Couldn't have lots of hair flying around if she was to look like a professional chef.

Having checked that she'd packed everything into her bag, Hannah said goodbye to her fellow back-packers and headed off to The Boardwalk Café, needing to pick up some breakfast and hoping to beg a lift from someone going her way. One good thing about being on the tourist track. People were usually generous about giving help. It was fun chatting about where you'd been and what lay ahead.

Optimism put a happy smile on Hannah's face. Today was going to be a great day. It was lucky she'd seen the job advertisement in the Cairns newspaper two weeks ago, lucky her résumé had won her an interview. If her luck held good—and why wouldn't it?—by tonight she would be the new chef on the top cat of the Kingtripper line.

''The phone. It is Antonio. For you,'' Rosita announced, carrying the cordless telephone to where Isabella Valeri King was enjoying morning tea by the fountain in the loggia.

Yesterday Isabella had celebrated her eightieth birthday. She did not feel eighty. Her hair was white, her skin more wrinkled than she cared to notice, but she could still sit with a straight back and her dark eyes missed very little of what was going on around her. Rosita, who had taken care of her needs for the past twenty years, had insisted she rest today, but Isabella's mind never rested.

Antonio…her second eldest grandson, thirty-two years old and too footloose and fancy-free for Isabella's liking. Something had to be done about that and soon. Time was the enemy as one got older. The young thought they had all the time in the world, but it wasn't so. It had to be used wisely and well, not frittered away.

"Thank you, Rosita." She smiled at her most trusted confidante and lifted the telephone to her ear. "What is the problem, Antonio?"

A call during the day invariably heralded a problem.

"Nonna, I need your help."

"Of course."

"I'm at Cape Tribulation. There's a management hitch at the tea plantation here. I'll have to fly down to the other plantation at Innisfail and fix things at that end. The problem is, I had today earmarked to interview three people who've applied for the job of chef on *Duchess*…"

Isabella's interest was instantly sparked. "And you would like me to do that for you and select the best?"

A huge sigh of relief. "Can do? I'll have them re-directed from the office at the marina up to the castle for you."

"It will fill in my day very nicely, Antonio."

"Great! They're all young women…"

Splendid, Isabella thought. Perhaps one might be a possible wife. Antonio would need someone who liked being on a boat.

"…and according to their résumés, which I'll have brought up to you, they've had years of experience in the catering business. What I specifically need is a chef who can cook fish really well. That's expected on *Duchess*. So make sure you question them on that, Nonna. Test them out."

She smiled at his confidence in her ability to do so. And why shouldn't he respect her judgement? She'd been supervising the catering for the weddings at the castle for many years and never had there been a complaint about the food served. Isabella had always insisted on the best and knew how to get it.

"You can safely leave this matter in my hands, Antonio. Go and sort out your management problem with a clear mind."

"Thanks, Nonna. I'll catch up with you this afternoon."

"Hannah O'Neill?" Speculative interest in the receptionist's eyes. "Lucky you're early. Unfortunately, Mr King is tied up with other business so I'm to redirect you to King's Castle where Mrs King will conduct the interview."

"Fine!" Hannah flashed an agreeable smile. "If you'll just point the way..."

Surprise in the receptionist's eyes. "You don't know King's Castle?"

Was she supposed to know? "I only arrived in Port Douglas a couple of hours ago. Still getting my bearings," Hannah quickly explained, throwing in an apologetic shrug. "Must say I headed straight for this marina. Great place..."

"Oh! Well, keep going along Wharf Street, on up the hill and you can't miss it. You'll see the visitors' parking area. The steps there will lead you to..."

A real castle! Hannah could hardly believe her eyes as she reached the top of the steps some fifteen minutes later. It even had a tesselated tower! Positively medieval! Although the colonnaded loggia that fronted the massive building could have been lifted straight from ancient Rome. A simply amazing place, set here overlooking the ocean in far North Queensland. A very commanding place, too.

Hannah's curiosity was instantly piqued. What kind of people owned it, lived in it? Only great wealth could maintain it like this, she decided, eyeing the manicured lawns and magnificent tropical gardens. There had to be some really interesting history behind it all, too. Maybe she could winkle some of it out of Mrs King during the interview. People did enjoy talking about themselves and the less talk focused on Hannah, the better.

It surprised her to see an elderly woman seated outside in the loggia. She looked perfectly relaxed, in command of a table placed near a very elaborate stone fountain. In front of her were several manila folders and a tray holding refreshments; a jug of fruit juice, another of iced water, a plate of cookies, three glasses. As Hannah approached, she realised the woman was subjecting her to a very thorough scrutiny. She also noted her autocratic air, the black silk dress and the opal brooch pinned at her throat.

Hannah had anticipated meeting a much younger woman, but she suddenly had no doubt that this was *Mrs King,* and while she might be a white-haired old lady, the mind behind those brilliant dark eyes was razor-keen. Hannah felt she was being catalogued in meticulous detail, from the wavy wisps that invariably escaped her plait, to the cleanliness of her toe nails poking out from her sandals.

She was suddenly super conscious of her bare midriff and wished she'd worn a skirt instead of the hipster jeans which might or might not be showing her navel. Looking down would be a dead giveaway of an attack of nerves. Hannah held her head high, shoulders back, spine straight, and blasted any negative judgement with her best smile.

''Hannah O'Neill?'' the woman inquired, a slightly bemused expression on her face.

''That I am,'' Hannah replied, employing an Irish lilt for a bit of friendly distraction.

A nod, a half smile. ''I am Isabella Valeri King.''

Which was definitely a mouthful of name, underlining a heritage that probably had royalty in its background. Being hopelessly ignorant of any useful facts, Hannah maintained her smile and warmly replied, ''A pleasure to meet you, Mrs King.''

Another regal nod. ''Please sit down, Miss O'Neill, and help yourself to any refreshment you would like.''

Hannah was glad to put the table between her and any possible sight of her navel. She wasn't usually self-conscious about her body, but then she wasn't usually in the presence of a woman who exuded aristocracy and was dressed like a duchess. Certainly not in these tropical climes.

She poured herself a glass of fruit juice, managing not to spill a drop, and determined not to be intimidated out of putting her best foot forward, even if it was only shod in a brown leather sandal. After all, hadn't the old Roman senators worn leather sandals in their villas?

"Quite fascinating the list of places where you've worked, Miss O'Neill," came the first leading comment. "Have you been travelling around Australia alone?"

"Well, not all alone. I've made friends here and there and sometimes journeyed on with them. It's good to have company on long trips."

"And much safer for a young single woman, I'd imagine. Or are you attached to someone?"

"No." Hannah grinned hopefully. "Still looking for Mr Right."

"With an eye to marriage?"

The highly direct comeback floored Hannah momentarily. "Well, I guess that's what Mr Right is for, Mrs King," she recovered, understanding this woman was highly unlikely to view the more casual live-together relationships in a kindly light.

"Unfortunately he's not all that easy to find these days," she rattled on, feeling she had to give a proper explanation of her failure to find him. "It's not only a matter of him being right for me. I've got to be right for him and then the timing has to be right..." She heaved a rueful sigh. "Here I am, twenty-six, and the whole combination has not yet occurred for me."

A sympathetic nod. "It's true one cannot order it. As you say, there has to be a combination of auspicious circumstances."

Got out of that one, Hannah thought triumphantly.

"Would you mind telling me something about your family, Miss O'Neill? I take it you are of Irish descent?"

Hannah laughed. Good humour covered a multitude of shortcomings. "Irish on both sides," she replied. "My mother's name was Ryan. Maureen Ryan. I'm the middle one of nine children, all of us very much wanted and loved."

"Nine? That's a very large family these days."

"I know. It amazes most people. Some disapprove, calling it breeding like rabbits. I can only say I've never felt like a rabbit and it's always been great having the ready support of a big family."

"You haven't missed them on this long journey you've taken?" was asked curiously.

"Well, we were brought up to be independent, too. To follow our own star, so to speak. Besides, they're all only a call away. I noticed an Internet café here in Port Douglas when I arrived. That makes it easy to stay in touch."

The old lady nodded, seemingly pleased with Hannah's portrayal of her family background. "Are you keen to have many children yourself when you do marry?" she asked.

Why was this important? Hannah sensed it was. "At least four," she answered truthfully, then shaved the answer with practical issues. "*If* I can get my husband to agree, *and* I'm not too old when I find him."

"Twenty-six, twenty-seven," the old lady said assessingly, as though she was totting up how many babies Hannah could fit in. "Perhaps you need to stay in one place for a while, Miss O'Neill. How long do you plan on staying in Port Douglas?"

"Oh, definitely for as long as the job lasts, Mrs King."

A warm approval was now coming from the older woman, which boosted Hannah's confidence. Family was obviously a key factor here. Hannah didn't care why as long as it was working for her. Her instincts were shouting— *Play it to the hilt!*

"I notice you spent the last tourist season working at King's Eden Wilderness Resort in the Kimberley,'' came the next tack in the interview.

King's Eden…King's Castle…oh wow! Was this another branch of the same family? More legendary stuff—the Kings of the Outback and the Kings of the Tropics?

''What did you think of it?'' Isabella Valeri King ran on.

Hannah's enthusiasm did not have to be feigned one bit. ''The resort was a fantastic slice of the Outback. A great experience. And so was working with the head chef there, Roberto,'' she popped in judiciously. ''I swear no one can cook barramundi like Roberto. Absolutely superb. It has to be the best-tasting fish in the world. Whenever the guests at the homestead brought in a catch…''

''And you learnt to cook it as he did?''

''Mrs King, give me a fresh barramundi, and I'll give you a meal to remember.''

''I may take you up on that, Miss O'Neill.''

Enough about cooking! That hook was in. Better to get back to family. She projected eager, bright-eyed interest. "Is there a connection between the King family here and the Kings of the Kimberley?"

"We are related," came the proud acknowledgment. "The older brother of my husband, Edward, carried the family line on at King's Eden."

Remembering the wonderful homestead on the great cattle station, sited like a crown on the top of a hill overlooking the river, she had to ask, "Did your husband build this castle?"

"No. My father did. It used to be known as the Valeri Villa in the old days. After my father died, and my son took over the plantations, the local people started calling it King's Castle, and so it is today."

"Plantations?" Hannah prompted.

"It was all sugarcane then." She waved to the view. "Look across the inlet!"

Cane fields stretching from the sea to the mountains.

"My mother used to watch the burning of the cane from the tower here. But they do not burn the fields now. The cane is harvested green with special machinery. My grandson, Alessandro, looks after that business. His brother, Antonio, manages the tea…''

"Tea?'' Hannah remembered seeing a tea plantation at Cape Tribulation.

Isabella nodded. ''Though I suspect Antonio is more interested in his Kingtripper Company. The new boat, *Duchess,* is his pride and joy.''

So Antonio would be her boss if she clinched the job. Antonio, Alessandro…a very strong Italian influence here. Maybe that encompassed the thing about family.

''Your résumé says you worked on a boat at Fremantle in Western Australia,'' Isabella went on, getting back to tricky business for Hannah.

She nodded. ''Catering for Sunset Cruises around the harbour.'' If you could call drinks and nibbles *catering!*

''So you're used to working in a galley.''

''Oh, yes. Absolutely.''

''And you don't get seasick?''

"Never have been."

True, but she hadn't been tested much on that score. Better buy herself some travel-sickness pills to be on the safe side.

"Matteo supplies a selection of exotic fruit for exclusive use on *Duchess*," Mrs King informed her. "You will have to learn about their qualities. Matteo is my youngest grandson. He looks after the tropical fruit plantations."

Three Kings, Hannah thought, and wondered if they had wives. "Do you have any great-grandchildren, Mrs King?"

She smiled, delight twinkling in her dark eyes. "A little boy, Marco. He is the son of Alessandro and Gina, who is now expecting another child."

"Well, congratulations!" Hannah said heartily.

"Thank you. Unfortunately, my other two grandsons have not yet found..." Her mouth quirked. "...Miss Right."

"It's not easy," Hannah said with much sympathetic feeling.

"Love is a gift," Mrs King murmured, with a look of satisfaction that stirred Hannah's curiosity again.

Before she could inquire what was meant they were both distracted by the noise of a helicopter zooming very close above them.

Mrs King looked even more satisfied as she explained, "That will be Antonio, coming in to land on the helipad. He said he would join us here if he could."

Uh-oh! Hannah's stomach did a little flip. She'd been doing so well with Mrs King, establishing a really warm rapport that would surely have led to her being given the job. Now she had to face the boss-man and win him over, too.

Double jeopardy!

At least she had his grandmother onside, which was some consolation, but undoubtedly the boss-man would have the last say.

Antonio…

Not married.

Did this mean he was hard to please? Or just too busy with his plantations and boats to care too much for any woman? Obviously a high-flyer in his helicopter, Hannah fervently hoped Antonio King would still have his head in clouds of tea business, at least until she could get a handle on him.

CHAPTER TWO

HANNAH'S heart did a hop, step, and jump as one of the great entrance doors to the castle swung open and *the man* came striding out towards the table by the fountain. Her wits went flying off to limbo in scattered little fragments. Her stomach contracted as though all her female muscles were twanging red alert. It was lucky she was still sitting down or her knees might have melted.

If this was Antonio King he was a king-size ten on the male Richter scale! Tall, dark and handsome did not sum it up. Dynamic energy came from him in waves. It had a magnetic effect that glued Hannah's gaze to him. She did manage to keep her mouth closed which stopped any danger of drooling.

He was dressed in light grey tailored shorts and a grey and white striped business shirt, collar open, sleeves rolled up. Both arms and legs seemed to bristle with athletic muscle power. He wasn't Mr Universe, but he was very, very masculine, the kind of masculine that made any woman want a bite of him. As many bites as he'd allow. Major sex appeal here! Major!!

"Nonna…" Arms out ready to embrace his grandmother, a smile full of straight white teeth, a squarish jawline, strong nose. "Thank you so much for filling in for me."

"My pleasure, Antonio," she said, rising from her chair to receive him with affection that was amply returned.

He enveloped her in a hug and planted a kiss on her forehead while Hannah was occupied admiring the taut cheekiness of his very cute backside, as well as the glossy thickness of his black hair and the neatness of his ears. Flynn's ears, she remembered, had stuck out, and she'd actually planned on giving her children plastic surgery to pin theirs back if they inherited Flynn's ears. Not that she had to worry about that anymore, but she couldn't help thinking Antonio's ears were quite perfect.

He swung aside from his grandmother, gesturing towards Hannah, a dazzling smile accompanying the question, ''And this is…?''

''Miss Hannah O'Neill,'' his grandmother supplied. ''Your third applicant for the job of chef onboard *Duchess*.''

''Hannah…'' He stepped forward, offering his hand, grey eyes with intriguing bits of hazel in them meeting hers with the impact of an atom bomb, blowing apart the long-held shield around Hannah's heart. ''…I'm Tony King.''

Tony, Tony, Tony…, some wild voice in her head sang as she stood up to greet him properly.

Hannah O'Neill sure had a body, Tony thought, noting her eye-catching curves as she rose from her chair. Didn't mind showing it off, either, the clingy midriff top outlining breasts that would very sweetly cushion a man's head, hipster slacks laying bare a highly feminine waist and a peek-a-boo navel with…was that a butterfly tattoo around it?

No time for a closer examination, though Tony found himself fancying precisely that. Satin-smooth skin, honey-tan, a nice soft roundness to her flesh, no bones sticking out, definitely the kind of feminine physique that appealed to him.

Her choice of clothes had probably turned his grandmother off, but they were a turn-on for guys. No question. A clever piece of calculation for this interview? Misfiring in these circumstances. A black mark against her would have been instantly notched in his grandmother's mind.

She lifted her hand to meet his and he automatically grasped it, actually feeling a little jolt of pleasure at the touch of her—a slender hand, long fingers, warm and soft. She smiled and he was momentarily fascinated by the dimples that appeared in her cheeks. Very cute effect.

Her eyes were green, like the green of forest pools. Thick fair hair waved from a centre parting and was pulled back in a plait, although she hadn't been able to trap it all. Fuzzy little tendrils gave her face a rather endearing frame that went with the little girl dimples.

"I'm very pleased to meet you, Mr King."

Nice voice, sort of musical.

"Tony," he corrected, without pausing to think if giving her his first name was appropriate.

"Tony," she repeated in a soft sensual lilt that put a tingle in his groin.

And those green eyes were dynamite, projecting a pleasure in him that could scramble his brains if he wasn't careful. Already he was thinking he'd like to taste the mouth that had spoken his name like that. He was still holding her hand. He clamped down on the urge to hold more of her—not the right time or place—though he had a strong desire to pursue this woman once the job issue was out of the way.

Good thing he could blame his grandmother for selecting someone else for the position of chef. Which he had no doubt she would do. It neatly separated business from pleasure. And he could probably wangle some other job in town for Hannah O'Neill if she wanted to stick around.

"Miss O'Neill is your new chef for *Duchess*."

"What?" The word spilled out before Tony could catch it back. He instantly released Hannah's hand and spun around to face his grandmother, frowning over her shock announcement. "You've chosen already?"

She smiled serenely at him. "You did leave the decision in my hands, Antonio. Miss O'Neill and I had been chatting for some time before your arrival. There is no question in my mind she will suit you very well."

"Oh, thank you, Mrs King!" Hannah flew past him and grabbed his grandmother's hands, pressing them effusively. "I promise I won't let you down. And any time you'd like me to cook a barramundi for you, just say the word and…"

Cook? Tony stared at the thick plait falling down to the delectable curve of her spine, which led to her even more delectable bottom, and couldn't see Hannah O'Neill in a galley at all. He could only see her in a bed…with him!

Yet, here she was, dressed in positively provocative clothes, somehow getting on like a house on fire with his grandmother who was smiling at her as though she was the apple of her eye, not minding at all being pounced upon and gabbled at by a woman showing her naked navel with a butterfly tattooed around it!

Tony was still trying to get his scrambled mind around this incredible state of affairs when Hannah turned back to him and grabbed his hand again, squeezing it in both of hers.

"I'll be the best chef you've ever had on *Duchess,*" she gushed, her eyes lit up like Christmas trees, lots of electricity sparking at him and pumping up his heartbeat. ''I'll learn everything that needs to be done double-quick. I promise you won't be disappointed in me, Tony.''

Tony... She was doing it again, making his name sound like something she savoured on her tongue. It was almost a French kiss. And he sure as hell *was* going to be disappointed if she was working for him. Mixing it with an employee would only lead to trouble. Right now, with her hands clasping his, he had a mental image of her body clasping another part of his anatomy which was already giving him trouble.

''I think we should sit down and talk about this,'' he said quickly, deciding that putting a table between them was fast becoming mandatory. Not only would it hide his physical discomfort but it would give him enough distance to view Hannah O'Neill in a business-like light. If that was possible.

''Oh, yes!'' She released his hand to clap her own. ''I need to know when you want me to start and...''

"All in good time," he instructed, waving her to the other side of the table.

She virtually skipped around to the chair he'd indicated, her exuberant spirits totally irrepressible and almost mesmerising. Tony had to wrench his gaze away from her to get himself settled on a chair and his mind properly organised to deal with this problem.

He shot a glance at his grandmother who had resumed her seat. Her complacent air niggled him. She should have taken more time over this, should have consulted with him first before handing the job to Hannah. That bemused little smile on her lips...had she been mesmerised into an impulsive decision? His steely-willed grandmother?

"Ah! Here is Rosita with afternoon tea!" she announced with warm satisfaction, obviously happy now to turn this into a *social* situation.

Tony gave up. Hannah O'Neill had somehow wormed her way into his grandmother's good books and she was now being given the ultimate seal of approval—afternoon tea with Isabella Valeri King in the loggia. He was going to have to run with this ball, whether he liked it or not.

His grandmother proceeded to play grand hostess, aided and abetted by Rosita who fussed around, making sure everything was to their liking. She even produced the carrot cake with the cream cheese and walnut topping—a sure sign the company rated five stars. He was definitely down the mine here without a tin hat to protect him.

Having accepted the inevitable, Tony pulled over the manila folder that contained Hannah O'Neill's particulars, and focused his mind on getting down to business. Pleasure was now out. Regardless of how strong the temptation, it was utter madness to get sexually involved with an employee. He had to keep Hannah O'Neil at arm's length. Though even the width of the table didn't feel far enough.

"I see we addressed our reply to your application, care of Mason's Shop at Cape

Tribulation,'' he started off, needing to establish a properly serious vein to this meeting.

''Mmm...''

He looked up to find her licking cream from her lips, and his stomach instantly contracted, hit by a bolt of desire so hard his mind was out for the count.

''I was picking up my mail there,'' she explained, once she had her sexy mouth composed for speech. ''I spent a couple of weeks exploring the Daintree. Such an amazing rainforest. Being in the midst of it was like being plunged back in time to when...''

''Yes,'' he snapped, cutting off her disturbingly lyrical voice. He picked up a pen and jabbed it at the form she'd filled out. ''So where are you staying at Port Douglas?''

She took a deep breath.

Her breasts rose distractingly.

''I haven't found a place yet. I only came down from Cape Tribulation this morning. For the interview. But I'll find somewhere before tonight. I've noticed there are loads of accommodation places here.''

Tony was gaining the fast impression Hannah O'Neill operated on a wing and a prayer. She wasn't *prepared* for taking on this job.

''*Tourist* accommodation,'' he pointed out. ''If you intend to stay the whole season…''

''Absolutely,'' she assured him. ''I'll look for something appropriate.''

''Where have you left your luggage?''

''I put it in a locker at the marina.'' She leaned forward, smiling an eager appeal for understanding. ''You see, it did rather depend on whether or not I got this job what I did next, so…''

Definitely a wing and a prayer, Tony thought sternly, battling not to drown in her eyes.

''You will need an apartment with a well-equipped kitchen,'' his grandmother inserted authoritatively. ''Antonio, until Miss O'Neill gets her bearings here, I think it best you put her in one of the guest apartments Alessandro keeps in the Coral King block."

"A guest apartment?" Tony eyed his grandmother, wondering if she'd gone stark raving mad. Hannah O'Neill was not family or friend. She was an employee, and hardly a highly valued one at this juncture! She hadn't even been on trial yet.

"I'm sure there'll be one that's not being currently used," came the unshaken reply. "It will give Hannah the chance to settle into her new job and time to look around for suitable accommodation."

So, it was *Hannah* now!

"This is very kind of you, Mrs King," the fair-haired witch chimed in, her dangerous green eyes obviously casting spells in all directions.

"A simple resolution to immediate problems," his grandmother declared.

"Right!" Tony agreed, knowing he was outgunned before he'd fired a bullet. Feeling constrained to fire other bullets before they could be diverted, he fixed a steady gaze on Hannah O'Neill and stated, ''Please understand you start this job on a trial basis. The people who pay for a trip out to the reef on *Duchess* are promised the best of everything. Any failure to deliver it, in any area of service on that boat, cannot be tolerated.''

''You mean...no second chances?'' A touch of anxiety.

''That depends on how large the blunder is. The odd mistake can be glossed over. Anything that spoils a day out...''

''Would be terrible!'' she exclaimed, looking appalled at the thought. Like quicksilver her expression changed, her eyes filling with eloquent earnestness. ''Any little problem I might cause, I swear I'll make up for it a hundredfold. I've never had any complaints lodged against me, Tony.''

He could believe it. She could probably get anyone to forgive her anything. In fact, before they knew it, they'd probably be helping her out of whatever fix she got herself in. Here was his grandmother, *giving* her prime accommodation, and every time she called him by his name, his heart did this weird curl which took his mind off what he should be concentrating on.

Was she going to be a hazard for the male members of his crew? What if the dive team lost concentration? She'd better stay in the galley where she belonged. No straying out on deck. At least his current chef on *Duchess* was gay, so she shouldn't disturb him while he familiarised her with the job she'd be taking over.

"Chris, the chef you'll be replacing, wants to leave at the end of the week, so it would be good if you could start tomorrow, learning everything you can from him before he takes off. He's been a top chef for us and I'm sorry to be losing him."

"Why is he going?"

"Personal problems." He sighed, giving vent to some of his frustration. Then with an ironic grimace, he added, "His partner is yearning for the more sophisticated scene in Sydney. Paradise has its limitations.''

''I'm sure I'll be *very* happy here.''

She twinkled so much happiness at him Tony's chest tightened against the barrage. He forced his gaze down to the papers in front of him. He couldn't even hope she might start yearning for city lights and fly out of his life. It was clear from her résumé she'd been working in tropical climates for some time— Broome, Darwin, even a six-month stint at King's Eden in the Kimberley. Port Douglas probably was a paradise to her.

''So what time am I to be at the marina tomorrow?'' she asked eagerly.

''Eight o'clock. *Duchess* leaves at eight-thirty and returns at four-thirty. You'll be provided with a uniform which is to be worn onboard at all times.'' Which should cover up her most distracting assets. He glanced at his watch. ''If we leave now, I can introduce you to the crew when they disembark this afternoon.''

She immediately leapt up from her chair.

The butterfly pulsed at him.

Tony closed his eyes for one tight moment and rose to his feet, turning to his grandmother and lining up his vision on her.

"Always in a rush, Antonio," she sighed. "You didn't eat anything."

"Sorry, Nonna. Had a big lunch," he excused, stepping over to kiss her cheek. "Thanks again for doing the interviews."

"Perhaps Hannah will tempt you with her cooking."

Her culinary expertise was very low on the list of temptations where Hannah O'Neill was concerned. "As long as she tempts our trippers, I'll be happy," he said, hiding his dark thoughts.

"Mrs King, I can't tell you how much I appreciate your kind consideration and the chance to do my best for *Duchess,*" came the fervent flow from the seductive voice, working some more magic on his grandmother who bestowed her most benevolent smile.

"I hope everything works out well, my dear. You must have afternoon tea with me again one day. I did enjoy our chat together."

"I'd like that, too, Mrs King."

Oh, great! Tony thought in high exasperation. Next thing you know she'd be invited to family functions and she'd be in his face all over the place. Apart from which, he now had to contend with Alex's and Matt's reactions to her being put into one of the Coral King apartments, free of charge. *His* employee!

Nonna had boxed him into a very uncomfortable corner. Somehow he had to work his way out of it without upsetting her and without getting himself into big trouble with Hannah O'Neill.

CHAPTER THREE

"Come this way. We'll take the jeep down to the marina," Tony instructed, setting a brisk pace along a path that led around to the other side of the castle.

Always in a rush, his grandmother had said, and Hannah could see what she meant. Her legs were working overtime keeping up with him. Her heart was racing, too. She hoped she hadn't bitten off more than she could chew with this job. Living up to Tony King's standard of excellence was a scary prospect. She was going to have to learn fast, even faster than he walked.

The jeep was parked next to the helipad. Hannah was used to the small bubble helicopters that transported guests at King's Eden Wilderness Resort. The one Tony King flew was a very sleek machine in comparison. Big

money. Big money everywhere she looked.
Could a million-dollar-man fall in love with a
cook?

Her mind fuzzed with the thought of happy
miracles. She shot him her best smile as he
opened the passenger door of the jeep for her.
Unhappily he didn't see it. His gaze seemed to
be trained on watching her legs swing in before shutting the door again, and he frowned
all the way around to the driver's side.

Business worries? she wondered. It was
probably a bit forward to ask, so she held her
tongue as they rode down to the marina. He
maintained a grim-faced silence until they
reached the Kingtripper office where he
handed her over to the receptionist with an ef-
ficiency that left Hannah feeling somewhat de-
flated.

"Sally, this is Hannah O'Neill," he said
with almost curt haste. "She will be our new
chef on *Duchess.*"

"Hey! That's great! Congratulations!"

Hannah didn't even get time to reply.

"Supply her with a uniform, give her all the information about our cruises, and let me know when the crew comes in. I need to catch up on the latest figures."

"Will do," Sally more or less said to his back as he headed towards a door that opened to a private office. His abrupt manner hadn't dimmed her brightness. She had a pretty, vivacious face, a very short bob of dark brown hair, and blue eyes that danced lively curiosity at Hannah as she aimed a grin at her. "Welcome onboard the Kingtripper line."

"Thanks." Hannah grinned back, then nodded to the now closed door, whispering, "Does he always move this fast?"

"Well, the chef situation is getting fairly urgent with Chris all upset about Johnny leaving," Sally confided.

"Who's Johnny?"

"His partner. Who threw an ultimatum at him last week and took off to Sydney. Follow him or else." A roll of the eyes. "Chris would be better off without Johnny, if you ask me, but I guess gay relationships are just as de-manding as any other.'' She grimaced. ''I took this job as therapy after divorcing my over-bearing husband. What about you?''

''Me?'' Hannah's mind was still buzzing through all these new bits of information.

''Well, you're obviously a stranger in town since you didn't know about King's Castle. Are you escaping from something?''

''More looking around,'' Hannah said blithely, realising Sally was a gossipy person and it paid to be wary of giving out too much before she knew the lay of the land. Besides which, the ex-love of her life had receded into the far distance since she had met Tony King. She could almost wish Jodie well of Flynn. Almost.

She pasted a smile over the niggling sense of betrayal and elaborated on her carefree theme. ''I wanted to get work here and stay awhile. It's a beautiful part of Australia.''

''Sure is,'' came the ready agreement. ''And the perfect base for bouncing off to other great places. Have you got accommodation?''

"Yes. All fixed up." A strong sense of discretion told her to keep quiet on that front, too, so she rushed on, "What I need now is all the info on *Duchess* and…"

"A set of uniforms," Sally said obligingly. "Come on. I'll fit you out and feed you facts."

They only had ten minutes before *Duchess* glided in to dock at the marina. They watched it from the double glass doors that opened out to the promenade deck. Even to Hannah who'd seen many expensive boats in Fremantle, it looked fabulous; a sleek, stylish, black and white catamaran that exuded power and luxury.

"By far the best," Sally said proudly. "Only launched last year. Air-conditioned saloon and bridge, the most up-to-date entertainment systems, walk-in easy water access for diving or snorkelling, and for you, a fully equipped galley, including an espresso coffee machine and a dishwasher." She gave Hannah a droll look. "No plastic plates on *Duchess*. It's all top class."

Hannah nodded, observing the stream of day-trippers emerging onto the wharf—the clothes they wore, the bags they carried, all classy casual gear. These were moneyed people who paid for the best and expected it as their right. They looked happy and satisfied, which meant the five-star service had not fallen short today.

She took a deep breath, refiring her determination to ensure her service didn't fall short of the standard Tony King wanted maintained. The strong need to please him—more, to delight him—went far beyond what she should feel for her employer, but there was no point in trying to deny he'd put a new zing in her life. She got an electric charge just bringing his image to mind.

"Does...uh...Mr King ever go out on *Duchess*?" she couldn't stop herself from asking.

"Oh, yes! He skippers it most Saturdays and Sundays. And also when it's chartered by a special party. We've had a few celebrities with their entourage wanting *Duchess* to themselves for a day. Tony likes to take personal care of VIPs. He's a terrific host, and of course, they spread the word to their friends. Best publicity we can get.''

Tony… Sally spoke the name so familiarly, Hannah reasoned it must be okay to use it in front of the staff. It was silly to suddenly feel awkward about it. It had felt right when they'd been at the castle. He just seemed to have distanced himself from her since they'd left his grandmother. But she was probably being over-sensitive where he was concerned, not wanting to put any foot wrong.

Today was Wednesday. She had two days to learn all the ropes, practise her cooking and have everything down pat before *he* came on board. Tomorrow she would bring a notebook with her and jot down everything Chris did, everything she had to know about the galley and how it worked. Once the overall routine was fixed in her mind, she could add her own special touches, show Tony he'd really got a prize in his new chef. Then he'd give her that heart-buzzing smile and…

"Crew's coming off now," Sally announced, jolting Hannah back to the immediate situation. "Eric and Tracy and Jai do the diving. They're the first three. Next comes Chris and his assistant, Megan, then the skipper, David, and the first mate, Keith."

Five men, two women, all of them young and looking very fit and full of vigour. Soon to be four men and three women, Hannah thought. She saw Chris—hair very peroxide blonde—hurrying past the others, an urgent intensity driving him as he headed for the office.

"I'd better get Tony," Sally muttered, and made a dash for his door.

He emerged just as Chris bounded in, clearly pumped up with his personal problems, his frown lifting as he saw Tony. "Did you get someone?" he burst out, so intent on his own needs he didn't even give Hannah a cursory glance.

"Calm down, Chris." The strong, authoritative voice warned the chef he was out of line. "You have just walked past the person I've hired as your replacement."

"Sorry, sorry…" He spun to face Hannah, relief breaking a smile through his anxiety. "Hi!"

"Hi!" she returned with smile inviting fellowship.

"This is Hannah O'Neill," Tony introduced. "Chris Walton, who'll show you precisely what's expected of the chef on *Duchess* over the next two days."

Which jerked Chris's head back to Tony. "Do I have to? Can't Hannah…?"

"No." Very firm. "You stay till the end of the week. As agreed, Chris."

"But Megan could show her everything."

"It's your responsibility." The grey eyes were very steely as he added. "Don't let me down, Chris."

Me, too, Hannah thought on a panicky note, her nerves instantly protesting the prospect of being thrown in at the deep end without a life raft.

"You now have a cut-off day," Tony went on. "You can book a flight to Sydney on Friday evening. You'll forfeit your pay and a reference if you leave before then. Understand me?"

Chris crumpled. "Yeah, yeah. I just thought…"

"I want a smooth changeover, Chris."

"Okay!" He sighed and turned back to Hannah. "Don't get me wrong. It's a great job. I just need to be elsewhere."

She nodded sympathetically. "I will appreciate your staying on to show me how to handle everything, Chris."

"No sweat," he muttered, but it obviously was. The absent Johnny definitely had the screws on him.

The others streamed into the office and having settled the departure issue with Chris, Tony proceeded to introduce her to the rest of the crew. They seemed a cheerful bunch and

Hannah felt only good vibrations coming her way, no reservations about her fitting the role she'd taken on.

She was very conscious of Tony watching, and hoped he was pleased with the quick and easy connections made and the positive mood engendered by them. In any tourist business, it was important to promote an air of friendly approachability. Keeping a happy face was second nature to Hannah and today it was very easy for her to exude happiness.

A lovely new place to explore.

A new job to keep her going.

A new man who might just be Mr Right...if her heart was telling her true!

"Hey! Great dimples!" David Hampson, the skipper remarked. He was the last one to be introduced, the senior man on the crew, and very good-looking with bright brown eyes and a charming grin which he swung from her to Tony. "I think you've picked us up an asset here."

It earned a frown. "What we need is great cooking."

"Granted," David cheerfully agreed, returning a sparkling gaze to Hannah. "But give it to us served with dimples and it'll put a fine edge on our appetites."

She laughed, liking his good-humoured teasing.

"Are you ready to move now, Hannah? Got everything you need?" Tony shot at her, cutting off the laughter.

"Yes." She quickly picked up the plastic bag which contained her uniforms and a pile of print-outs on the Kingtripper cruises.

"Right!" He addressed the crew. "I expect you all to look after Hannah tomorrow, without her becoming a distraction to what you should be doing. Just keep everything running smoothly. Okay?"

They chorused assent.

His gaze sliced to her. "Let's go. I'll take you to your accommodation now so you can get settled and ready for work in the morning.''

''See you all tomorrow,'' she tossed at everyone and quickly accompanied Tony out to the walkway through the shopping mall, her heart fluttering at his rush to be on the move again.

''Where's your luggage?'' he asked.

''This way.'' She waved to the left and he was off at a stride that demanded she keep up. A glance flashed at his profile told her his mouth was grimly set again. ''Thanks for your support back there,'' she said tentatively, grateful for his stand with Chris.

''I hope you're not going to be trouble, Hannah,'' he grated out.

''Trouble?'' she echoed, flustered by this negative reading which she hadn't been expecting.

He beetled a warning look at her. ''David Hampson is married. He's got two children.''

''Well, that's very nice for him,'' she replied, still mystified by the almost accusing manner.

''Yes. Let's keep it that way.'' His chin jutted forward, along with his gaze as they walked on.

It took a while for his meaning to filter in. Tony King saw *her* as a threat to David Hampson's marriage? Why on earth would he think that? Because David had made a comment about her dimples? That was ridiculous…wasn't it?

''You know, it's not my fault I've got dimples,'' she said testingly. ''I was born with them.''

''And a lot else, besides,'' he muttered darkly.

It was too much for Hannah. ''Do you have a problem with me?''

''No.'' His chin jutted even more forward. ''Why would I have a problem?''

''I don't know.'' She frowned over the puzzle. He'd been distant towards her ever since… ''Maybe if you'd been making the choice, I wouldn't have been given the job.''

"I have the utmost faith in my grandmother's judgement," he declared as though not the slightest doubt had ever entered his mind.

"Well, that's a relief!" She heaved a sigh to get rid of that bit of unnecessary tension. "It's not a good feeling working for someone who doesn't want you."

"No question that I *want* you," he said very dryly.

"That's okay then." She felt much better, and to relieve any worries he might have about her, she said, "Generally I get on very well with people."

"So I noticed."

"And I don't believe in messing with anyone's marriage." *Not even Flynn's and Jodie's.*

"I'm glad to hear it."

"I certainly wouldn't enter into any flirtation with David."

"Fine!"

"Sally filled me in on Chris's situation so I understand about that, but is there anything else I should know about the crew so I don't put a foot wrong?"

"Nothing that springs to mind."

"You're not going to warn me off Eric or Jai or Keith?"

"Tracy might well throw you to the sharks if you get your teeth into Jai." A sharp glance. "Do you fancy him?"

How could she fancy any of them with *him* around? Didn't he know he outshone them by about a million megawatts? "I thought they were all attractive people, but they didn't ring any special bells for me," she answered honestly.

"Who knows when the bell might toll?" he said with heavy irony.

It tolled the moment you walked into my life, Hannah thought, but she wasn't sure Tony King was ready to hear that, particularly when he seemed to have some funny ideas about her...like she was some kind of honey-pot who drew men from other women. Which was really strange, because no one had ever cast her in the role of femme fatale before. She wondered why he saw her that way?

A happy thought struck. It had to mean he found her attractive. Maybe more than just attractive if he thought other men could be tempted out of their relationships because she was there.

No question that I want you.

What if he actually meant *he wanted her* in a man-woman sense, not a job sense? Excitement pumped her heart faster. It almost put a skip in her step as they exited from the mall and headed towards the row of storage lockers outside another booking office. Hannah quickly found hers, unlocked it, and lifted out her backpack.

"Is that all?" Tony asked as she closed the door on the emptied locker. He looked amazed at the economical amount of her possessions.

"It is easier to travel light," Hannah explained matter-of-factly.

He stared down at the bag near her feet as though it represented a life he couldn't quite bring himself to believe in. His gaze shifted to her well-worn sandals, then slowly travelled up her much-washed and somewhat faded jeans. He was probably realising she had few clothes with her and they were in frequent use, but this direct re-appraisal made Hannah super-conscious of her body again.

Her knees quivered. Muscles below her stomach spasmed. By the time his scrutiny reached her bare midriff, she could feel her nipples hardening in some wild anticipation of his liking the shape of her breasts, even wanting to touch them. His gaze certainly lingered on them long enough to take her breath away. She couldn't think of anything except how much she wanted him to really *want* her, and her temples were pulsing with an exhilarating excitement when he finally looked into her eyes.

But there was no suggestion of desire in his. No flirtatious twinkle.

What poured out at her was an almost savage intensity of feeling. It gripped her heart like a vice, squeezing it as though he wanted to extract her life essence, everything she was made of. Not because he wanted it. He just wanted to know. And he was angry at the need to know.

Hannah could feel herself shrivelling inside. She didn't understand what he found wrong with her, why he was angry. In sheer self-defence, she broke the shattering flow from him by bending over to pick up her bag. He beat her intention by grabbing the straps ahead of her.

"I'll carry it for you," he said gruffly.

She didn't argue. In fact, she snatched her hand back from making any contact with his. When he set off for the parking area where he'd left the jeep, she lagged a pace behind, struggling with a mountain of emotional confusion. She wasn't sure she wanted to go with him or be connected to him for any length of time.

Rejection hurt.

She'd been there before.

All those months with Flynn…then to find him cheating with her best friend. It had made everything—absolutely everything—feel wrong.

She'd only just met Tony King but…anger started to burn, searing away the hurt. He had no right to treat her as though she was some kind of unwelcome intruder in his life. He could have vetoed his grandmother's judgement and taken on one of the other applicants for the job of chef. She shouldn't be fretting over what he might perceive as *wrong with her.* The fault obviously lay in him.

She was fine.

His grandmother thought she was fine.

The crew of *Duchess* thought she was fine.

So there had to be something wrong with Tony King if he didn't think she was fine.

CHAPTER FOUR

TONY tried to get a grip on himself as he drove the jeep up to Macrosson Street. He'd never felt jealous over any woman in his entire life. Just a harmless comment about Hannah's dimples and David Hampson could have been a dead man back there, which was a totally over the top reaction.

The effect Hannah O'Neill had on him was getting close to disastrous. Even when she had set him straight in an upfront reasonable manner that should have forced him to be rational about the crew situation, he couldn't get over the hump of the feelings she stirred in him. He told himself it was stupid to transfer those feelings to every guy who met her. She wasn't so…stunningly captivating. She was just… very attractive.

Yet when he'd checked her over again with that one modest backpack from the locker telling him she was certainly unique amongst all the woman he'd known—living with so little—bells had definitely been ringing for him, a whole host of physical bells that still had his body buzzing with demands he had to dampen, not to mention the alarm bell in his head that told him he was in danger of losing it, along with all the common sense he'd learnt from past experi-ence.

Remember Robyn, he savagely recited to himself as he spotted a place to park and pulled the jeep into it. He'd taken the tempting bait, fallen into the Robyn trap, then found she was claiming special privileges from the crew on the grounds of being *his woman,* lording it over them and even being rude to the day-trippers because *she* didn't have to please anyone as long as she was pleasing Tony King in bed.

No more of that.

Employees could not be playmates.

Never!

He switched off the engine and steeled himself to look at Hannah O'Neill with no more than polite consideration.

"I have to pick up the apartment key from my brother. It will only take a few minutes." He pointed to the building he was about to enter. "That's the control centre for King Investments. Alex runs it. Are you okay waiting here?"

She nodded, her attention turning to the building so he only caught a glimpse of the bewitching green eyes. He got himself moving, determined on swift practical action. The sooner Hannah was delivered to an apartment, the sooner he could get her out from under his skin.

A pity he wasn't involved with anyone at the moment. That was probably half the problem, missing the intimate company of a woman he liked. There was a hole in his life to be filled, but that was no reason to fill it with Hannah O'Neill. It was just a matter of looking around, putting himself in the social swim. He'd find a woman who attracted him and maybe she'd be right for him. Like Gina was for Alex.

Now there was a marriage he could envy. His brother had hit the jackpot with Gina Terlizzi. And made a lucky escape from the woman who'd thought she had Alex right where she wanted him—a user like Robyn. Self-centred sexy women could be very dangerous. A man definitely needed to keep his wits around them.

He just caught Alex as he was about to leave. Five o'clock. No working overtime now he had Gina to go home to. "Hold on a moment! I need a key to one of the guest apartments," Tony told him, blocking the doorway out of the executive office.

His big brother backtracked to his desk, throwing him a questioning look. "I didn't know we had anyone arriving."

"We don't." He heaved a sigh and rolled his eyes. "Nonna, in her wisdom, has offered an apartment to my new chef for *Duchess* until she gets herself settled in Port Douglas.''

''She? You're replacing Chris with a woman?'' Raised eyebrows. ''I thought you preferred a male chef.''

''Chris has worked very well, but he did put me in a bind to get someone fast and there were only female applicants.'' Sighing his vexation over the whole pressure situation, he went on to explain, ''I asked Nonna to interview them and she seems to have taken a real shine to this Hannah O'Neill. Gave her the job before even consulting me about the others.''

''Accommodation, too,'' Alex remarked, smiling at Tony's obvious chagrin.

''I just hope she's not a free-loader who'll prove difficult to shift once she's in,'' Tony muttered darkly.

''Oh, I'd trust Nonna's judgement on that. Very astute when it comes to character,'' Alex drawled, fishing a key out of a drawer.

''Character has nothing to do with the over-all picture,'' Tony argued. ''I don't like *any* of my staff getting preferential treatment, let alone a newcomer.''

Alex shrugged. ''If it's only a stop-gap...''

''Nonna even invited Hannah to afternoon tea in the loggia. And asked her to come again.''

''So?'' Alex's sharp blue eyes were highly amused at this preferential treatment. ''Aren't you always telling me to relax and go with the flow?''

Tony heaved a sigh of exasperation. Alex had always been into controlling things. It seemed that being the oldest brother he'd been over-endowed with a sense of responsibility and he was big enough and tough enough and smart enough to carry through anything he thought should be done. Over the years Tony had tried to lighten him up. Turning those tables on him now was simply not appropriate.

''This is work, Alex, not play,'' he tersely reminded him.

''If Nonna thinks it will work out fine, I'm sure it will,'' he blithely returned, tossing over a key attached to the Coral King tag. "I take it this Hannah O'Neill is...uh...very appealing?"

"As far as I'm concerned she's completely out of bounds. Thanks for the key." He turned to leave, then hung back on a strong afterthought. "Don't mention this to Matt."

"Why shouldn't I mention it to Matt?"

"Because..." He didn't want his younger brother sniffing around Hannah. She wasn't Matt's employee. He'd feel free to pursue an interest in her and...

"Well?" Alex prompted, looking quite intrigued.

The conflict he was struggling with could not be voiced. "Just leave well enough alone. As Nonna should have." Holding the key between finger and thumb, he shook it at Alex. "She's gone too far with this."

"I imagine she was just trying to give you a smooth changeover, Tony," came the bland reply. "Do you have Hannah O'Neill parked downstairs?"

"Yes, she's waiting in the jeep."

"Then I'll walk out with you and meet her. Give you my opinion."

"That isn't necessary," Tony grated, wishing he hadn't run off at the mouth.

"I'm curious. As you say, it's not every day Nonna takes such a personal interest in someone she's just met."

At least Alex didn't have eyes for anyone but his wife, Tony reasoned, giving up on arguing. This brother probably wouldn't even notice Hannah's dimples. He certainly wouldn't look as far as the butterfly!

Hannah noted the display window of a real estate agency just along the street. As soon as she had some spare time, she'd inquire there about available accommodation for residents. She was tempted to do it right now, but it would probably be a black mark against her if Tony King returned and didn't find her waiting in the jeep. Besides, her backpack couldn't be left unattended in this open vehicle. It was not a good move to risk losing what she had, including her new job.

Tony King's confusing attitude towards her was very unsettling. She wished she hadn't accepted his grandmother's offer of the Coral King apartment, even with the understanding it was only on a very temporary basis. While it was too late today to change her mind on that issue, she would certainly assert her independence as soon as possible.

Her nerves tightened as she saw him emerge from the building in step with another man who was undoubtedly his brother, coming to check out the unheralded *guest* his grandmother had insisted on accommodating. Alessandro…Alex…

He was bigger and taller than Tony, though there was no mistaking the family likeness in their strong facial features. Same thick black hair, too. The way they carried themselves held an innate confidence that somehow exuded success in whatever they did. Both very striking men, Hannah thought, yet it was Tony's presence that made her heart slip beats.

Sure she was about to be introduced, Hannah opened the passenger door of the jeep and hopped out, feeling the need to stand her ground in the face of being judged again. The action instantly drew attention from Tony's brother who took one sweeping glance at her and then smiled, apparently seeing no wrong in her at all.

"Hannah, this is my brother, Alex. Hannah O'Neill."

Alex's eyes were a vivid blue and Hannah felt warmth and kindness flowing from them as he offered his hand. "Welcome to Port Douglas, Hannah," he said in a deep pleasant voice that contrasted sharply with Tony's curt tone.

She smiled back, relieved at *his* ready acceptance of her. "It's good to be here." The touch of his hand was nice and warm, too, comforting. "I hope I haven't caused a problem,'' she added earnestly. ''I can find some other place to stay.''

''As I understand it, Tony's rushing you straight into work, so I'm perfectly happy to go along with my grandmother's arrangements.''

''Thank you.'' Needing to establish she had no intention of becoming a problem, Hannah quickly added, ''I promise I won't impose on your generosity for long.''

''Don't worry about it.''

Alex withdrew his hand and clapped his brother on the shoulder, grinning widely as Tony shot him a sharp look. ''You've got the key. I'll leave you to handle everything. Happy days!'' he added, saluting both of them as he moved off about his own business.

''What a nice man!'' Hannah remarked on a sigh of pleasure in the meeting.

''Alex is married.''

The emphatic warning tightened up her nerves again. What did Tony think she was? Some kind of man-eater? ''I know that,'' she stated, glaring considerable impatience at him. In fact, enough was enough on this point. "Mrs King told me so. She also told me he has a son and his wife is pregnant. Should that stop me thinking he's a nice man and she's a lucky woman?"

He grimaced at her irritation, looking quite irritated himself. "I was merely giving you information which I didn't think you had."

"Thank you," she bit out, reminding herself he was her new boss and while he might be the most exasperating man alive, she didn't really want to get on the bad side of him, so she climbed back into the jeep, vowing to keep her mouth firmly shut in his presence except for saying "Thank you," when it was appropriate.

He settled himself beside her and said, "I'll drive you down to the apartment now."

Hannah wondered where it was but limited herself to replying, "Thank you."

It was only a three-minute drive. The jeep pulled up outside an apartment block situated on the lower side of Wharf Street. She'd walked past it earlier this afternoon on the way up to the castle. The apartments were terraced down the hill to the waterfront and all of them would clearly have a fantastic view of incoming and outgoing boats, not to mention the sunset which would start happening soon. Great location!

Despite her earlier misgivings about accepting this very hospitable offer, Hannah couldn't stop her spirits rising at the thought of spending her first few days in Port Douglas at a place that had such marvellous advantages. It was close to the township, close to the marina, and being a ''guest' apartment, it would undoubtedly provide pure luxury after her weeks of bunks in back-packer hostels.

She followed Tony down a path which led straight to one of the top floor apartments. He was carrying her bag with no visible effort which showed just how strong his muscular arm was…and his muscular back and muscular buttocks and muscular legs.

She sighed, wishing he wasn't such an enigma. Was he *off* women for some reason? He'd been curt with Sally, too, so maybe it wasn't just her.

If he'd had a bad experience—and Hannah certainly knew how *bad* experiences felt— well, being sour on women in general could be quite understandable. It did wear off after a while. Though learning to trust again was difficult if one had been brutally let down by someone near and dear. The shields went up and no one was allowed close.

A wounded man, Hannah thought, feeling a rush of sympathy for Tony King as he unlocked the door and waved her to enter ahead of him. "Thank you," she said warmly and smiled to show she harboured no ill feelings about his manner towards her. After all, he didn't know her very well...yet.

He stiffened into a very upright stance as she sailed past him. Hannah kept going, giving him some space to feel more comfortable with her. A galley kitchen led to a big open living area, furnished with a dining and a lounge setting—all cane with brightly coloured cushions in a cheerful tropical pattern.

"This is lovely!" she cried, forgetting to limit her speech to "Thank you' as she beamed her pleasure back at him.

He lowered her bag onto the floor. Refraining from any comment on her comment, he pushed the Coral King tag attached to the door key into a slot on the wall. "This turns on your electricity and the air-conditioner."

"Thank you," she said, clasping her hands gratefully and hoping he didn't think she'd been too effusive about a place which was strictly temporary.

He stared at her for several seconds and Hannah caught the sense he was in some fierce conflict with himself. "Right!" he finally snapped. "I'll leave you to it then. Don't forget it's an eight o'clock start tomorrow."

"I'll be there on the dot. Probably earlier just to be sure. You can count on it," she assured him.

"Good!" He nodded but his head was the only part of him that moved. He seemed stuck there in the doorway, his gaze still locked on her, like he was trying to burn his way into her mind to see if she could be trusted.

"I'll keep everything here spick-and-span. You don't have to worry I'll make a mess of it."

"I'm not worried," he asserted, frowning over her supposition. "I'd better give you my card so you can contact me if you run into any problems. The mobile phone number can always reach me."

He started forward, taking his wallet out of his back pocket and opening it to extract a business card. Hannah also moved forward to meet him halfway, anxious not to hold him up since it was clear he wanted to get away. He was looking at the card, stuffing his wallet back in his pocket and walking so fast he almost collided with her.

Shock on his face.

His hands instinctively grabbed her upper arms to steady her as she rocked back from him.

"Sorry..." The word rushed out of her mouth, just before her throat completely choked up as shock hit her, as well.

His face was so close his eyes seemed to blaze into hers, and the fingers pressing into the soft flesh of her arms...they seemed to burn, too. She felt invaded by an electric current that was playing total havoc with her entire body.

Heat was swarming through her like a giant tidal wave, making her senses swim, filling them with a huge awareness of the man holding her, the overwhelming maleness of him tugging at her own sexuality, the strength he emanated, the power, even the masculine scent of him was flooding through her nostrils, an intoxicant that jammed all thought.

She stared back at him, her mouth still half open though incapable of emitting sound. Her ears seemed to be roaring with other messages…a million bells exultantly ringing that he wanted to do far more than hold her arms, far more than tunnel into her brain to find out who and what she was. There was no reason at all in what sizzled from him but its sheer physical blast held Hannah totally captivated.

His gaze dropped to her parted lips and the certainty he was going to kiss her clutched her heart. His head started lowering towards hers, then unaccountably jerked up. For one shattering moment she saw horror in his eyes. The hands on her arms sprang open, releasing all contact. He shook his head, stepped away, bent and scooped up the card that had fallen on the floor.

Hannah was too dazed to move a muscle. He lifted one of her hands and pressed the card onto her palm, actually curling her fingers around it. ''There!'' he said on a heavy expulsion of breath. ''Must go now. Must go. Number's on the card if you need me.''

His fingers brushed her cheek as though driven to draw her out of what had happened between them and into the immediate *now*. "Okay?" he asked, the horror in his eyes replaced by anxious alarm and a need to paste something else in place.

She nodded, still unable to get her throat to work.

"Okay," he repeated, backing off, swivelling around, heading straight for the way out.

He was gone with the door closed behind him before Hannah could even blink. She found herself touching her cheek as though his fingers had left some imprint there.

She'd never felt anything like this before.

Not even with Flynn, whom she'd loved.

Tony...Tony King.

CHAPTER FIVE

SHE hadn't called.

Tony brooded over this absence of any contact with Hannah O'Neill as he drove to the marina on Saturday morning. For the past two days and three nights he had been more conscious of having his mobile phone on hand than he'd ever been, waiting for Hannah to test his response to her, anticipating her voice almost every time it rang. Part of him had wanted it to be her voice. At least then he could have dealt with a real problem instead of being subjected to this continual inner restlessness.

He'd even taken his mobile to the party he'd attended in Cairns last night—just in case she called—and fully intending to let her hear the party sounds in the background so she'd know he was out enjoying himself and not thinking of her. And he'd meant to enjoy himself, too. Except he couldn't stop thinking of how *she* made him feel and not one woman at the party had lit the slightest spark of interest in him.

The inescapable truth was he wanted *her*. Only her. It didn't matter what his mind dictated, his body was in full rebellion against all restrictions where Hannah O'Neill was concerned. He'd barely caught himself back from kissing her on Wednesday afternoon, and he strongly suspected he wouldn't have stopped at kissing, given they'd been in the apartment with a bed handy.

Unless, of course, she'd said no.

Which she might have.

She certainly hadn't called.

Tony kept telling himself he should be pleased about that. It proved she did not intend to take any advantage of her power to get at him. Or maybe she was simply waiting to check out his behaviour towards her today. Which should be exemplary—treating her as he would any other staff member, making a few allowances for her newness on the job—except he wasn't sure how far he could trust himself to act as he should.

He could only hope she wouldn't have such an undermining impact on him today. The surprise element was gone. When he saw her again, he might very well wonder why he'd got himself into such a twist about her. He'd probably been blowing the whole thing up in his mind because…well, he wasn't used to being struck so strongly by any woman. It had never happened before.

Tony decided he didn't like it.

A guy was supposed to be in control, knowing exactly what he was doing and why. He had to stamp his authority on this situation. Be captain of his own ship.

This resolution burned in his mind as he parked his jeep and checked his watch. Five past eight. The whole staff should already be on board *Duchess,* preparing for the day ahead of them and their passengers. He strode down the wharf, feeling a swell of pride in his newest acquisition to the Kingtripper line. This cat left all the others for dead, not only in speed but in looks and amenities.

And Hannah O'Neill had better live up to his grandmother's judgement when it came to cooking seafood! If she didn't dish up the best barramundi he'd ever eaten, then nothing about her could be trusted.

He greeted the catering people who were just leaving *Duchess,* having delivered the day's order of fresh salads and bread rolls. At least that much of the guaranteed sumptuous lunch was reliable, he thought, stepping on board to more greetings with the dive team who were checking equipment against a passenger list.

"How many coming with us?" he asked.

"Thirty-six," Tracy answered. "Almost a full complement."

The limit was forty. Thirty-six meant a busy day for all hands, especially Hannah's as people drifted in and out for lunch.

"How's our new chef fitting in?"

"Hannah is amazing!" Tracy declared with a little shake of the head denoting awed admiration.

"Doesn't miss a trick, that girl," Jai remarked with a nod of agreement.

"It's the energy she gives out," Eric said more consideringly. "Lots of positive vibes. Gives everyone a good buzz while she gets 'em doing what she wants."

Aha! Tony thought triumphantly. So that was how she'd got his grandmother in! Hannah O'Neill was a witch weaving spells and she'd caught him in her magic trap before he'd built up any objective immunity. *Amazing* was right. Everyone was giving her what she wanted—the job, free accommodation, approval all around, and she'd probably wanted to be kissed, too.

"What about her cooking?" Tony asked.

"Don't know," Jai answered. "Chris was doing it yesterday."

"I think she was helping until she started the exotic fruit thing," Tracy chimed in.

"Yeah! Now that's what I mean," Eric said pointedly. "She got everyone having fun tasting all that stuff. I reckon Hannah could sell anything if she put her mind to it."

"No worries, Tony," Jai assured him with a grin. "Even if her cooking isn't great, she'll sell it to them with her smile and they'll *think* it's great."

"I hope you're right," Tony bit out, feeling he'd been an all too easy victim of that smile.

"Hey! Don't forget that scrumptious salad she brought along yesterday," Tracy reminded the other two divers. "Anyone who can create a salad as good as that is sure to be a fine cook."

Tony frowned. "She doesn't have to bring salads with her."

Tracy shook a finger at him. "Don't discourage it. I sneaked back for seconds it was so yummy. And I wasn't the only one. The stuff we get delivered didn't rate in comparison. Wait and see, Tony."

"Okay. I'll wait and see. I'm glad you're all happy with Hannah. I'll go and have a word with her."

"A lot more cheerful to be around than Chris has been the past few weeks," Eric tossed at him for good measure.

All of which formed a very positive picture, Tony acknowledged as he moved on into the saloon. The need to be fair-minded about Hannah O'Neill, particularly where this job was concerned, bore down on the personal prejudice he'd been nursing. There was not a hint of envy or anything negative coming from Tracy, and while Jai and Eric obviously *liked* Hannah as a person, neither guy had given any indication of hot sexual interest.

Was he the only one turned on by her?

Energy…chemistry…all he really knew was that some compelling force was being generated and he needed to get a hold on it so it didn't mess him up. Captain of his ship, he thought again as he approached the L-shaped bar that enclosed the galley. Consciously relaxing, he was ready to smile at both Hannah and Megan who were busily setting out cups and saucers for the first rush on tea or coffee by the incoming passengers.

''Good morning, Tony!'' A bright greeting from Megan who spotted him first. She had a very short crop of brown hair and was into ear-piercing in a big way—at least a dozen studs and rings hanging off her lobes—but Tony didn't mind her taste in fashion. Nothing about Megan distracted him.

''Good morning,'' he echoed, barely managing a glance at her. His attention was riveted on Hannah, who was very slow to raise her gaze to him.

There was tension in her sudden stillness. Her shoulders squared as her chin lifted, eye-lashes at half-mast, veiling her feelings until she had them guarded enough to deflect any probe from him. He caught the wary expression instantly. And more. A flash of vulnerability that made his stomach flip.

She was as unsettled by him as he was by her.

No devious plan.

The thoughts flashed through his mind and a wild satisfaction surged over the questions that had nagged so infuriatingly. It wasn't one-sided. He wasn't her victim. A bite had been taken out of her breezy confidence with that almost-kiss on Wednesday, which surely meant she'd been left in some sexual turbulence, too. *Over him.*

It put a grin on his face.

"Hannah..." he said with an encouraging nod, not stopping to consider whether *encouraging* was a good move.

She had her hair braided again. Such long, thick wavy hair had to look fantastic when it was not constricted, even more fantastic spread across a pillow. Funny how both she and Megan wore the same uniform—white T-shirt and shorts with coral cuffs and the Coral King insignia on the pockets—yet it simply looked neat on Megan. Hannah filled it with luscious curves. Tony had a mental image of the hidden butterfly and wondered if it was fluttering.

''Got here in time!'' a triumphant voice declared behind him.

A voice he instantly recognised.

Matt's voice!

His younger brother swung past him and dumped two trays of fruit on the wide counter of the bar. ''Hi, Tony!'' he tossed over his shoulder, the barest acknowledgment before concentrating the full blast of his big personality on Hannah. ''You must be the new chef. I'm Matt King. I supply the exotic fruit you ran out of yesterday. And from what Chris said, if you want a job change...''

''Stop right there, Matt!'' Tony cut in. ''Hannah is mine!''

''Hannah...'' Matt rolled her name off his tongue with obvious pleasure and completely ignoring Tony, thrust his arm over the bar, hand extended. ''Glad to meet you!''

She took his hand, looking at him somewhat dazedly. Matt was almost as big as Alex and always a hit with women, an uninhibited talker with the gift of the gab, not to mention his good looks, curly hair, and dark chocolate eyes that apparently had the power to induce swooning.

Tony unclenched his jaw and bit out, "If you think you can come in here and poach on my territory…" He stepped right up to the bar in belligerent challenge, which served to unhook Matt's hand from Hannah's so he could hold it up to Tony in a gesture of peace.

"I know you need her right now with Chris leaving," he said reasonably. "But…"

"No buts. You've delivered your fruit. Now beat it, Matt!"

Both hands up now, warding off the firepower Tony was in no mood to tone down. "Okay, okay," Matt soothed. "Didn't mean to make waves. Just letting Hannah know I appreciate her talent for getting people to try something new. Not many people have that kind of entrepreneurial skill, Tony. It takes…"

''What does it take to get you moving out of here, Matt?''

He huffed. ''You're not listening to me.''

''You're out of line.''

Lowered brows, eyes shooting some private meaning. ''Alex said...''

''I don't care what Alex said,'' Tony snapped, wishing he hadn't implied to his older brother that Hannah was more Nonna's choice than his and he didn't like being boxed into a corner.

''I thought...''

''Think again.'' And Alex should have kept his mouth shut!

''Fine!'' Matt slanted an appealing smile at Hannah. ''Just keep up the good push on my exotic fruit. Could tap into new markets with the kind of people who go out on *Duchess*.'' He clapped Tony on the shoulder. ''Got the word. No poaching!''

He swaggered off in such apparent good humour, Tony knew he'd just been baited. His younger brother was too damned clever, and he enjoyed nothing better than getting a rise out of Tony or Alex. It probably came from having been bossed around by them when he was little, but Matt really needed being taken down a peg or two. In the meantime, he'd better stay clear of Hannah if he didn't want to get thumped.

With a sense of having settled something important, Tony swung his gaze back to the woman who'd triggered this territorial battle. In his mind she now belonged to him. It had been a swift transition in his thinking about her but Tony didn't pause to ponder reasons or gather doubts. How they were going to get over the employer/employee hump was still a complicated issue. Nevertheless, there had to be a way.

The green eyes were opened wide, staring at him as though she didn't know what to make of his sharp exchange with Matt. Hot colour in her cheeks indicated a fast pumping of blood. Had she picked up the inference that he'd complained to Alex about their grand-mother's arbitrary choices?

"First day without Chris," he rolled out, us-ing business to remove the personal element from her thoughts. "Let me know if you run into any problems and I'll do what I can to ease them for you. Don't try to go it alone. Teamwork is always better. Okay?"

She nodded, still wide-eyed and looking to-tally confused.

He moved off to greet the passengers now streaming onto *Duchess,* a new zest for life leaping happily through his veins. His confu-sion had smoothed out into an understanding he found both exhilarating and highly chal-lenging. It was great to feel captain of his ship, master of his fate, the holder of knowledge he could use as he saw fit.

He wasn't expecting to be rocked again.

Fate decreed otherwise.

CHAPTER SIX

HANNAH is mine!

The possessive ring of those words had been so loud and strong, nothing else had really penetrated Hannah's mind during the brief meeting with Tony's brother, the tropical fruit plantation King, Matt...Matteo... more Italian-looking than Tony or Alex, his eyes so dark they were almost black, reminding her of his grandmother.

Tony had cut him off so fast, she'd only had an initial impression of big vitality, then... *Hannah is mine!* Was it simply a territorial demarcation, brooking no interference with his staff placement? Or was it as personal as it had sounded? Intensely personal.

She'd been incredibly nervous about coming face-to-face with Tony this morning. Having watched and assisted Chris for the past two days, she was reasonably confident of handling the job. That wasn't the problem. It was the feeling that Tony King had the power to stir things in her she had no control over which really threw her into a loop.

Physical attraction was fine. It was natural. Mutual attraction made it all the more exciting. But chaos had never been acceptable in Hannah's world. She liked to plan, to have her life proceeding in an order that made sense to her, that resulted in foreseeable outcomes. Of course, one had to make reasonable allowances for the unpredictable, and she'd always been able to adjust quickly to external surprises. But she'd been well and truly rocked by the internal shocks Tony King had left her with on Wednesday afternoon.

Hannah is mine!

Did he sense he could just take her if he wished?

It was a terribly disturbing thought. She wasn't just a body that responded willy-nilly to his. She needed to get some respect going here. There was a little matter of freedom of choice, too. Tony King did not *own* her, not even as a chef. Being on trial went both ways. She could leave if she wanted to.

Though when it came to *wanting,* she couldn't help thinking he looked stunningly handsome in his white and navy captain's uniform. Most of the incoming female passengers obviously thought so, too, glowing as he greeted them on entry to the saloon, then casting an interested second glance at him as they advanced to the bar for tea or coffee.

"A terrific host," Sally had said, and certainly he was giving out pleasure as though he had an endless well of it to give. In fact, Hannah was beginning to feel quite jealous of the smiles he bestowed so easily on other women. She remembered his first smile to her up at the castle, before his grandmother had declared her the new chef for *Duchess.* Definitely pleasure. But he'd withheld it from her ever since. Which begged many questions and didn't make her feel good.

Nevertheless, she put on a happy face for the people she was serving, automatically feeding their anticipation of having a wonderful day ahead of them and fully intending to contribute to it every way she could. It wasn't her fault that the smile froze on her face at the sound of a voice she'd never wanted to hear again.

''Hannah! I can't believe it! What on earth are you doing here? I thought you must have taken some top-flight job overseas...''

Jodie! Her ex-best friend, Jodie Dowler. Who was now Jodie Lovett, Flynn's wife. Which meant... Hannah's heart dropped like a stone at the thought of Flynn being on board, too.

Here was Jodie almost at the bar, her long black hair still styled into a sexy tousled look with artistic strands hanging around the darkly pencilled blue eyes, bright red lipstick matching a bright red shirt, gold belt, tight white slacks—gorgeous Jodie, babbling loudly about Hannah having completely dropped out of *the scene.* Had she always been so *loud?*

Tony was frowning, his gaze darting between the two of them, and Flynn was bound to appear next—Flynn, the dazzling dynamo of the money markets, whip-lean in his city elegance, sharp, witty, one of the few men Hannah had ever known to carry off chestnut-red hair with distinction, with an arrogance that somehow made it highly individual to him, setting off his high forehead, but not hiding his ears, Hannah reminded herself. Though that detraction didn't help to lower the rush of inner agitation. She wished there was a hole in the ground for her to drop into.

''Not a word of you from anyone for the past two years,'' Jodie complained, as though Hannah had committed a crime against *her.*

''Tea or coffee?'' she asked through gritted teeth.

"Hannah?" It was an exasperated appeal for some personal acknowledgment to be made.

"Fruit juice…soft drink?" The words tripped out in stubborn denial that Jodie *Lovett* had any claim on her apart from the service she was paying for.

"Oh, coffee then," she gave in petulantly. "Make it two cappuccinos. Flynn will be here in a minute. He just stopped to chat to the dive team."

Hannah concentrated on using the coffee machine, fiercely cursing the fact she was a captive audience here in the open galley, but be damned if she'd give Jodie or Flynn any response that wasn't related to her job. She didn't care if it appeared rude. They'd lost any right to demand anything more personal from her two years ago.

"Hannah, for God's sake! We were best friends…"

It hadn't stopped her from having sex with Flynn behind Hannah's back.

The coffee whooshed into the cups.

"We didn't plan to hurt you," Jodie hissed.

"Help yourself to sugar." Hannah nodded to the sugar bowl as she placed the order on the counter in front of Jodie, determinedly keeping her hands steady. She was shaking inside, hating being cornered like this, hating Jodie for confronting her so publicly, hating herself for not being able to deal with it better.

It was like ghosts walking over her grave—the grave of the life she'd had before it had been killed by Jodie and Flynn. She didn't want to remember it. It was gone. Long gone. They had no right to come back and haunt her with it. She'd moved on.

"Damn it! I'm not going to let you block me out!"

Selfish. Totally selfish. What Jodie wants, Jodie gets. Except she'd coated her selfishness with lots of sugar in the old days, so sweetly cajoling Hannah had been fooled into closing her eyes to that truth. Much easier to go along with Jodie's plans, to fit in. But not today. Not anymore. Ever.

''Flynn and I are only human, Hannah,'' came the slimy defence. ''If you hadn't been up on your high-flying pedestal, not making time for us...''

''Please excuse me. There are other people to serve.''

''The other girl can serve them,'' was snapped back at her.

Hannah ignored that argument, skirting Megan to move to the other end of the L-shaped bar where there were people waiting, wonderful strangers who had no axe to grind. She bestowed her best smile on them.

''Tea or coffee?''

''Tea, please.''

Thank heaven she didn't have to move back to the coffee machine. The urn for tea was at this end. ''Is this your first visit to The Great Barrier Reef?'' she asked brightly, picking up the woman's very English accent.

"Yes. Though we have dived in the Caribbean," her husband remarked.

Hannah grinned. "Ah...but what we have here is one of the seven wonders of the modern world. I'm sure you won't be disappointed."

They laughed and took their tea. "I'll report back to you," the man tossed at her as they left the bar.

"You do that," Hannah cheerfully invited, wishing they'd stayed to chat longer. It was easy to give out to strangers. She had a desperate need to surround herself with them. Then she could keep operating on a surface level that didn't hurt. But Megan was serving the only other person waiting.

"Flynn, Flynn..."

Jodie's call was like a nailfile scraping her spine.

"...look who I've found! It's Hannah!"

She would not turn around. No way. She picked up the bowl of used teabags and emptied it in the garbage bin.

"Hannah?" Flynn's voice sounding puzzled and disturbed.

Hannah hoped a load of guilt was hitting him like a freight train and he'd want to get out from under the weight of it as fast as he could.

"Come and say hello to her," Jodie commanded, a note of sweet malice in her tone now, determined on breaking Hannah's guard against them.

"Ah, Jodie, isn't it?" Tony's voice. "I was just inviting Flynn up to the bridge to watch us take *Duchess* out now that everyone's on board. You have your coffee? Yes, I see you have. Good! Do come and join us."

A very smooth rescue mission.

Hannah hated his awareness of a problem blowing up with her at the centre of it, but was intensely grateful for his interference.

"Thank you," Jodie crooned. "But Flynn must say hello to Hannah first. We haven't seen her for so-o-o long."

Putting her on the spot in front of her boss!

No ready excuse to deny a simple greeting.

No escape.

Flynn had to be faced.

Get it over and done with, Hannah savagely reasoned.

Her stomach was curdling with rebellion as she swung around, her gaze instinctively targeting Tony, the green blaze of her eyes warning she was not going to play Jodie's game, come hell or high water.

"It's good to see you, Hannah," Flynn said quietly.

He was a blur beside Tony—a grey blur in some grey outfit—and she kept him a blur. Tony was taller, broader-shouldered, physically a stronger male image that helped to blot out Flynn's, and his eyes were certainly just as sharply intelligent, boring into hers for answers that were buried under too many layers of pain to be dragged out into the open.

She forced herself to nod at Flynn but she wouldn't speak to him. Wouldn't look directly at him, either. She didn't care if Tony fired her on the spot. Her eyes challenged him to do it if he wanted to. Everything within her revolted against pretending this situation was acceptable in any shape or form.

''Right! Let's move,'' Tony said with firm authority, picking up the two cups of coffee, thrusting one at Jodie and one at Flynn so they were forced to take them. ''Hannah has a lot to do preparing for lunch and it's a fine morning to be up on the bridge. Come and enjoy the view.''

He literally herded them away, talking at them with so much dominant energy, any protest they might have made wilted under it. Even so, Hannah knew Jodie wouldn't be silenced for long. In no time flat she'd be spilling out to Tony that his new chef was a very *new* chef, her major work experience being in a completely different field. And then she'd pump him for all he knew about her— ammunition for her next visit to the galley.

"What a pushy bitch!" Megan commented.

Hannah took a deep breath to ease the painful tightness in her chest. The sense of being intolerably trapped was pressing in on her. The urge to run, to jump off the boat before it left dock, warred with the responsibility she had taken on. Impossible for Megan to handle all the work of the galley alone. The others had their duties. She'd be letting everyone down if she skipped out on them.

"Are you okay?" Megan asked, concern in her voice.

Hannah looked at her, desperation voicing a plea. "Could I ask a big favour of you, Megan?"

"Keep between you and them?"

She nodded. "They caused me a lot of grief in the past."

"Leave it to me. You just do your stuff, Hannah, and I'll spike their guns every time they front up to the bar."

"Thanks." She managed a wobbly smile. "I'd really appreciate it."

"Be a pleasure. Though I don't think you need worry too much. Tony caught the drift and he'll cut them out of the pack."

"Cut them...what do you mean?"

"Oh, he has a way of spotting trouble-makers and diverting trouble before it can develop. The guy is really smart, you know? Not just a pretty face?"

A nervous little laugh gurgled from Hannah's throat. "I haven't thought of Tony King as pretty."

Megan grinned. "You mean...more a knock-out hunk? Gotta say he's not bad for an older guy."

"Not bad," Hannah agreed, wondering precisely how old Tony was. Early thirties? The phrase, "older guy" hadn't even occurred to her. On the other hand, Megan was only nineteen, making the age gap bigger.

"Anyhow, you just relax now," the younger girl advised. "You won't see those two again until lunchtime, and you can bet your boots Tony will be right on their tails, making sure you don't get hassled out of focusing on cooking. *Duchess* is his baby, you know. Got to have the food and everything else for it just right.''

''A hard boss?'' Hannah queried, worrying now that she might not measure up under the stress of being accessible to Jodie and Flynn. Did they have to keep spoiling everything for her?

''No. He's very fair. You can count on that. He expects you to be fair to him, too. That's okay in my book.''

Hannah nodded, though she bitterly wondered if there was any fairness in this world. Why did Flynn and Jodie have to visit Port Douglas at this time and book a trip on *Duchess* today of all days? If they had any decency, they'd stay away from her. Just let her get on with this job since it was her choice. They'd certainly made their choice.

Amazingly that seemed to happen. Or Tony King made it happen. They made no re-appearance in the saloon at all, not even for lunch. Keith, the first mate, brought down an order for three lunches of barramundi and salad. Hannah cooked the fish, Megan served the salads, and the lunches were taken up to the upper deck, along with a chilled bottle of Chardonnay.

''See?'' Megan commented smugly as she helped Keith stack the tray. ''Tony's got those two eating out of his hands. No problem.''

Except what they might be giving him in exchange, like personal information Hannah would prefer to keep private. She was utterly powerless to stop that and the thought of her past history being laid bare—especially to Tony King—made her feel vulnerable on too many levels.

It took considerable willpower to keep herself operating on a professional level, chatting to the passengers, ensuring what they ordered was cooked to perfection, delivering with a smile. Her inner tension eased somewhat once the lunch rush was over. No mishaps. No complaints. No problems apart from those in her head.

The afternoon wore on. *Duchess* left the outer reef at three o'clock for the run home. Most of the passengers trailed into the saloon, their scuba-diving and snorkelling finished for the day. Hannah forced herself to repeat the exotic fruit presentation which formed a pleasurable and refreshing wind-down during the ninety minutes it took to get back to Port Douglas. Tracy and Jai offered to man the bar and serve drinks, freeing Megan to take samples of the fruit to the upper deck.

Nothing was actually said, but Hannah sensed the whole staff had been worded up to shield her from the Lovetts. Ironically, this probably meant Flynn and Jodie had received five-star service all day, watched over and handled with kid gloves. All Tony King's doing, of course, though Hannah was under no delusions she'd be paying for it, one way or another.

If Jodie and Flynn didn't pounce on her the moment she walked off *Duchess,* Tony would, wanting to know what else in Hannah's background might raise an ugly head to disturb the smooth running of his ship. She tried not to think about it until she had to. Maybe everything could be avoided, relegated to the past where it belonged.

It was a vain hope.

They docked at the marina on schedule. The passengers streamed off, heading for transport back to their accommodation. The crew cleaned up after them. When there was nothing left to be done, they moved as a group onto the wharf, ready to report back to the office and be briefed on tomorrow's passenger list.

Predictably, Tony fell into step beside her, waving the others ahead to ensure a private conversation. Hannah's nerves jangled an instant protest, but her head told her she owed this man for saving her from an unbearable situation today, regardless of whether it had been simply a pragmatic decision to avoid a bad scene that might upset people who'd paid for pleasure.

A grateful "thank you" pushed to be said, yet it was an admission that led straight into territory she didn't want to tread. An apology did the same thing. Better not to say anything. Let him lead into the raw area, if he had to.

"Are you planning to skip out on me, Hannah?"

The question startled her into halting. Her head jerked up as the realisation hit that the last previous sight he'd had of her today was the confrontation over the bar when she had been on the verge of bolting. She met a hard piercing gaze that was determined on nailing her down.

Her own sense of fairness forced a reply. "No. I'm sorry about today. Those people..." The heat of acute embarrassment burned up her neck and into her cheeks. "...they're not likely to book another trip on *Duchess*."

"Right now they're sitting at a table out on the deck of the Fiorelli Bistro and Bar, which we'll be passing on the way to the office. You are being targeted, Hannah. I can keep them from getting to you but I'll need your co-operation. Are you willing to go along with me? Yes or no?"

"Yes." The word tumbled out, driven by an anguish of spirit that begged to be free of any further involvement with Flynn and Jodie.

"Then take my hand now and leave everything to me."

She didn't really take it. He took hers with a confident command that pulled her along with him. Another rescue mission, she thought, too shaken by the prospect of having to confront Jodie and Flynn by herself to even consider resisting Tony King's offer of support and protection.

It felt good, having him at her side.

She could feel his strength pumping up her arm, giving her wrung-out heart a much needed shot of adrenaline. Her frazzled mind didn't even begin to consider what Tony might do to ensure she wasn't harassed. He'd said to leave everything to him and her instincts had no trouble believing he would be master of the situation, whichever way it turned.

CHAPTER SEVEN

TONY liked the feel of Hannah's hand in his. He liked having her trust, too. What he didn't like was her reaction to the couple whose appearance on *Duchess* this morning had killed her natural exuberance stone-dead. Worse. She wouldn't even glance at the guy, and it had looked to Tony as though she'd been on the verge of quitting to escape the sense of entrapment with those two.

No need to be Einstein to work out the equation—*if he wanted to keep her, keep them out of her way.*

No need to consider his response, either. Losing Hannah O'Neill at this point was not acceptable. Not only would he be without a chef who had already won the approval of the crew, but he hadn't yet had the chance to explore what there could be between them on a personal level.

Nevertheless, this extreme stand from Hannah raised many questions that had Tony's mind buzzing, particularly since it hadn't softened one bit in the intervening hours of being free of the Lovett couple. Her current tension over their nearby presence was just as strong as it had been this morning. Which brought him to one firm decision. There was something going on here that *he* didn't want to walk away from.

It had been a very interesting day, observing the interplay between the Lovetts. No love left in that marriage. Tony doubted there ever had been love. The woman was a man-eating sexpot, mixing manipulative flirting with sly sniping, neither of which hit their mark with her husband who had maintained an air of arrogant boredom towards her malicious game-playing.

Tony had brushed off Jodie Lovett's questions about Hannah, stating only that she held the position of chef on *Duchess*. Flynn Lovett had bluntly told his wife to "put a gag on it" when she'd started claiming that Hannah's being a chef was ridiculous. He'd given Tony his full co-operation in diverting the conversation onto other subjects, much to his wife's chagrin. Yet Tony was convinced Flynn had been playing his own game—a waiting game—and the focus of all the games today was Hannah.

Why was the big question.

And why would she want to run away from them?

He could only think that old wounds had been re-opened. Bad wounds. Bad enough that re-visiting them was intolerable.

Tony didn't like that, either.

He wanted the butterfly flying free with him, not pulled away and hurt by these people.

"We won't take the usual route along the promenade deck to the office," he instructed. "We'll walk straight ahead into the shopping mall, bypassing the open-air table they've selected." Without pausing a beat he added, "For someone who's not a trained chef, I'd have to say you have a fine touch with barramundi.''

She darted an apprehensive glance at him and he grinned at her. ''You delivered. That's what counts. Now smile back at me. We're going to have a happy chat and not even notice the Lovetts.''

Her smile flashed out, tinged with relief at his acceptance of her. ''I have had training, Tony. Though not anything formal. More like an apprentice.''

''Best training of all,'' he approved, pleased she could still say his name with that spine-tingling lilt. ''What's more, everyone on the crew likes you. You're amongst friends, Hannah.''

''They're a nice bunch of people.''

''True. I picked them myself.''

Her eyes flashed irony. ''Except for me.''

''You're certainly the surprise package but I'm not about to give you up. They're watching. Beam me another bright smile.''

She did.

"You've got killer dimples, Hannah O'Neill, and I want to hear you laugh."

She managed it, chasing away the hunted look his warning had briefly evoked.

Having twigged that her quarry was heading towards the mall doors instead of the promenade, Jodie Lovett grabbed her husband's arm, urging action. Flynn unfolded himself from his chair, waving to catch attention. "Tony, come and have a drink with us. Hannah, too."

The fingers Tony held instantly scrunched up, nails biting. It was disturbing proof that Flynn got to her more than Jodie did—Flynn, the man! And this was not the past. This was here and now. The idea of any man having a strong effect on Hannah stirred all Tony's hackles.

He did not so much as slacken their pace towards the mall, though he acknowledged the call by raising his arm in a farewell salute. "More work to do. Enjoy yourselves."

Which brought Jodie to her feet, fighting against having their plans frustrated. "Join us when you're finished," she pressed.

"Other plans," he cheerfully excused.

The doors opened.

As they reached the relative safety of the mall, closing out the Lovetts who would make themselves ridiculous chasing after them at this point, Tony was acutely aware of Hannah's shoulders sagging in relief. He decided not to comment. He had a strong suspicion she was not home free yet. All his instincts were telling him she had become a strong focus of discontent between the Lovetts today and they were not the kind of people to accept having their own interests frustrated.

They were used to winning.

But they were on Tony's home ground. So was Hannah. And Tony had no intention of losing. He'd take the battle right up to them if he had to. The hand in his gave him the right to do it and he was not about to let that right slip. Not for a moment. Not while ever Flynn Lovett was in town!

Hannah's knees were like jelly. But any chance of a forced meeting with Jodie and

Flynn was now behind her so at least she could breathe freely again. She took a big gulp of air and shot Tony King a genuine if somewhat wobbly smile.

''Thank you for escorting me.''

His eyes lightly teased. ''I quite enjoy the role of white knight to fair maiden in distress.''

Very conscious that she had put him to considerable trouble on her account today she promised, ''I'll be fine tomorrow.''

He squeezed her hand. ''Let's get through today first.''

It reminded Hannah there was still work to be done and she had to get her mind focused on what needed to be ordered to cater for tomorrow's trip. She didn't think of extracting her hand from Tony's. He didn't release it, either, until they reached the office and they went about their separate responsibilities. Only then did she realise how deeply comforting that physical link with him had been.

Over the past two years she had become accustomed to conducting her life on her own.

She hadn't minded being alone. It was easy enough to seek company when she wanted it. Strange to recall now how wary she had been of Tony King's effect on her this morning. It was different, feeling he *cared* about her. Or maybe it was just the job he cared about, making sure she didn't let him down.

Somehow that didn't matter. He had held her hand when she had needed it held and it had felt good. Better than anything she'd felt for a long time.

Having completed the salad and seafood orders for Sunday, and feeling more positive about her job now that Tony had been so decisive about keeping her on—pleased by her cooking, too—Hannah set her mind on tomorrow as she prepared to leave the office. She didn't have to think about Jodie and Flynn anymore and she wouldn't. Tomorrow would not be darkened by the past. Tomorrow she would see more of Tony King who might be the man to blot Flynn out of her memory on every level.

Mr Right…

Now there was a piece of whimsy, she thought, given how wrong she'd been about Flynn wearing that title. Still, one could but hope. Better than wallowing in old mistakes.

"Hannah!"

Her heart jumped. Tony was coming out of his private office, obviously wanting some last word with her. She paused, nervous tension gripping her again at the thought of being queried on her connection to Jodie and Flynn.

"I'll drive you home," he said with serious intent. "See you safely to your door."

She stared at him, realising he thought there was a possibility of her being accosted by the two people she wished to avoid. It didn't seem likely to Hannah, yet…they had been waiting for her to come off *Duchess*.

"It's only a ten-minute walk," she started to reason.

"A two-minute drive," he returned pointedly. "And not out of my way. I have to drop by the castle. My grandmother will want to know how you're doing.''

He didn't allow for any further argument, asking Sally to lock up the office and sweeping Hannah out to the car-park with him. The reminder of his grandmother's part in her current situation was exercising Hannah's mind as they settled in his jeep.

''Sally said I have Monday and Tuesday off,'' she quickly mentioned, once they were on the road. ''I'll find some accommodation for myself then.''

''There's no big hurry,'' he said offhandedly, as though her staying in the Coral King apartment was of no concern to him.

Had she taken a completely wrong impression of his attitude last Wednesday? Needing the issue clarified, she said, ''I thought you would prefer me out as soon as possible.''

He slanted her a look that seemed to simmer with personal re-assessments, setting her pulse skittering and re-igniting a very strong sexual awareness of the physical attraction she'd tried to put at a sensible distance.

"I'd prefer you to feel settled in Port Douglas," he answered. "Take your time in finding what's right for you."

They were reasonable words, especially in the light of her urge for frantic flight this morning. On the surface of it, he simply wanted to remove sources of anxiety, give her a bit of space, yet she felt he was now closing the distance he had put between them at their first meeting.

On the other hand, maybe she was just being super-sensitive, a nervous hangover from the stress of the encounter with Jodie and Flynn. "That's very kind of you," she said quickly, flushing self-consciously as she felt impelled to add, "You've been very kind all day. I do appreciate your help and...and consideration."

He pulled the jeep up on the verge of the road in front of the apartment block and Hannah rushed to alight. "Don't switch the engine off. I'll be fine from here. Many thanks again, Tony.''

Her feet hit the ground.

He switched off the engine.

It thumped into her heart that the last word had not been said and this driving her home was meant to lead to something else. The plain truth was... Hannah wasn't ready for anything else. She recoiled from giving any explanation of her reactions today, and her feelings for Tony himself swirled in an ambivalent mess. She shot him a desperate look of appeal, only to find his focus not on her at all.

His gaze was on another jeep—a common form of transport in Port Douglas, particularly with the hire-car companies. It had just passed their parked vehicle and was moving slowly up the hill towards the castle. It came as a very severe jolt to Hannah to see that the male driver had chestnut hair and his female companion's long black locks fell over a red shirt.

''They followed us!'' The shock of it spilled out the all-too-telling words.

"Yes!" Tony shot her a fiercely determined look. "No argument, Hannah. I'm coming in with you."

He was out of the jeep, his door banged shut in emphatic purpose before she could gather any wits at all. Her mind was in a ferment over the ramifications of Jodie and Flynn now knowing where she could be found in her private time.

As Tony rounded the jeep, she had the sense of a torrent of dynamic energy coming at her, encompassing her in his personal force-field. His eyes had the glitter of battle in them and his strong male face wore a hard aggression that was not about to countenance any denial of his intention.

Her knees had gone to jelly again. She felt helplessly caught by elements she had no control over and all her mind could do was bleat, *It's not fair…not fair…*

Tony scooped her along with him, an arm around her waist clamping her to his side. Somehow her legs kept up with his strides and they were at the front door of the apartment so fast, she then had to fumble in her handbag for the key. The moment it was produced, Tony took it, opened the door, and swept her inside. He was right behind her and she heard the door click shut, trapping her into what was now an inescapable situation.

"Okay!" he said with satisfaction. "When the Lovetts drive back down the hill, as they must, they'll see the empty jeep and conclude I'm here with you, so I don't anticipate they'll want to intrude because it's not me they want contact with."

It was impossible to refute his reasoning. Hannah felt sick at being pursued like this. What more did Jodie and Flynn want from her? Hadn't they taken enough, abusing everything she'd given them? She looked bleakly at the man who had appointed himself the safeguard between her and them. His eyes were ablaze with a demand for answers. The only words she could think of to say were, "It's not my fault."

His expression softened to sympathetic concern. "I think a stiff drink is in order. You go on out to the balcony and breathe in some fresh air while I raid the complimentary bar. What would you like?"

"I usually only drink water. It's good for you," she added so stiltedly, it brought an ironic smile to the grim set of Tony's mouth.

"Okay. A long glass of iced water coming up."

"Thank you."

Better to keep a clear head than fuzz it with alcohol. There was no possibility of drowning her sorrows in it anyway. She had a few minutes' respite before Tony's questions would start. With the feeling of having her privacy terribly violated and being helpless to stop it, she walked towards the setting sun outside, knowing it couldn't give her the sense of peace that this fraught day was finally over.

"Hannah…"

She paused, her spine tingling at the soft call. Not yet, she silently begged. Please…not yet. She couldn't bring herself to look back, to face what had to be faced. Not yet.

"I have to know the problem in order to fix it," came the quiet assertion. "Make up your mind to share it with me, Hannah, because it needs to be fixed. I'm not about to leave this apartment wondering if you'll still be here tomorrow."

How do you fix something that's unfixable? she wondered, moving on to unlock the glass door to the balcony and slide it open.

How do you handle people like Jodie and Flynn who won't recognise that the unfixable can't be fixed?

She stepped outside and wandered slowly over to the railing, leaning on it, gazing out over the water, the cane fields beyond it, the mountains beyond them, the reddening sky leaching colour from both sea and land.

Impossible to roll back the forces of nature, she thought. Everything moved to a pattern as old as time. Perhaps people did, too, and there was no stopping it.

Every female instinct in her entire body quivered as she heard Tony King step out on the balcony. He brought with him a force of nature that was far more immediate than those forming the landscape in front of her. It was coming right at her, and it was not about to be rolled back, either.

CHAPTER EIGHT

Tony set the drinks down on the glass top of the aluminium table on the balcony. There were six chairs around the table but Hannah hadn't chosen to sit. In fact, she'd distanced herself from him as far as she could, standing at the railing, her back still turned to him, shutting him out.

Was she brooding over Flynn Lovett, wishing...?

No, damn it! Whatever had gone on between them it was two years in the past and the guy was married. Not happily but that wasn't the point. Tony didn't want Hannah to be vulnerable to any move Flynn might make on her. He wanted that guy wiped right out of her mind. And talking about him wasn't going to do it. Her feelings about someone else was not what Tony wanted Hannah to share with him.

His instincts were raging at him to act.

Act now.

No waiting.

No weighing up rights and wrongs.

Talking, even thinking, was not the path to take here. Some things went beyond reason, he told himself, his legs already taking the path of their choice. Some things had to be pursued, known, taken in and processed. Some things could not be denied.

''Hannah...''

She turned her head towards him. The lost look in her eyes caused an intolerable tightness in his chest. It was wrong. She wasn't alone, wasn't lost. He was here. He had to get through to her.

Her skin prickled at the way he said her name—like an intense claim on her that threatened any resistance with the power to smash it. It struck a compelling need to understand what drove Tony King and drew her into turning from the railing to face the oncoming force.

Before she had time to understand anything, his arms were around her and her hands were flat against his chest and her lower body was in vibrant contact with his, completely blowing all awareness of the rest of the world right out of her mind. Hard muscular thighs pressing, a broad hot chest heaving against her palms, strong arms maintaining possession, eyes blazing into hers, intent on burning away any defensive barrier she might fling up.

No time…

His mouth crashed down on hers, starting a passionate onslaught of kisses, and some fierce wild creature burst into life inside Hannah, exulting in the passion, feasting on it, and far from flinging up barriers, she wilfully and wantonly incited an escalation of this tumult of feeling, a totally reckless exploration of it, driving Hannah's hands up over wonderfully muscled shoulders which she fancied could bear any weight, carry any burden and make light of it, revelling in the strong column of his neck, the springy thickness of his hair, the sheer dominant manliness of him that was geared to fight any battle for her.

And her breasts were now crushed against the thump of a heart that cared about her, wanted her, his hands telling her so, his body telling her so, banishing the loneliness, bringing her in from the cold of not having anyone for herself, giving her the sense that nothing could come between her and this man. He wouldn't let it. No other woman. Her...only her.

A deep primitive satisfaction seized her as she felt his erection pressing its urgent need to join with her, proof of how much she was desired, and the desire to have him was exploding through her, pounding a need that screamed to have the emptiness of her inner world filled by him.

Thumbs hooking into her shorts and panties, hauling them down, her own hands attacking his shorts, wild to be rid of obstructions, hot for the feeling of flesh against flesh, and the fierce elation of finding how big he was, her fingers wrapping around him, loving his arousal, anticipation of how he would use it playing sweet havoc with her own sex, the yearning so intense, so overwhelmingly needful.

He hoisted her up on the railing, one arm supporting her there as he moved between her thighs. She threw her arms around his neck, instinctively hanging on to his strength as she felt him slide between her soft folds, stroking, seeking, teasing, building the wanting to fever-pitch. She felt herself convulsing in readiness and wrapped her legs around his hips, desperate to pull him inside her, to have him there.

The first plunge came—oh, such ecstatic pleasure—and stayed deep, the whole hard length of him so deliciously deep, like an integral part of her that she'd always missed and been waiting for and here it was, making her entire body pulse with joy. Then he drew her head back from where she'd rested it near his ear and kissed her, invading her mouth with the same deep intimacy, and he scooped her off the railing and carried her with him still inside her, making her feel an integral part of him *he* couldn't bear to let go.

He unclipped her bra, lowered her to the table surface, rolled up her T-shirt, bared her breasts and kissed them with an intensity that seemed to draw on all she was. Her body throbbed to the rhythm of his mouth, incredible sensations flooding through her, and when he raised his head and looked into her eyes, it was as though he was piercing her soul, demanding entry, forcing entry with a power that would not be denied.

"Come fly with me!"

Another command—ringing in her ears this time, like bells of jubilation—and a hand stroked her stomach, circling the butterfly she'd had tattooed around her navel as a symbol of freedom from all the stress of her life before she flew away from it. But the only freedom she wanted now was the freedom to fly with this man, to soar to heights that only they could share, and she felt him move inside her, a slow slide out, a fast slide in...pause... her muscles squeezing, holding.

Again...and again...her whole body instinctively fine-tuning itself to his rhythm...and the soaring began, like wings lifting through her, beating faster and faster, carried on currents that ebbed and flowed, lifting, floating, lifting higher to exquisite pinnacles of feeling, then flying higher still until it seemed the magical sky they were travelling shattered in a starburst of sensation and she lost herself in it.

But she didn't stay lost because Tony gathered her up again... Tony...cradling her against his lovely warm chest, taking her with him and she was kissing his neck, tasting his skin, breathing him in—such a wonderful, beautiful man who hadn't stopped wanting her.

He laid her on the bed and swiftly removed the rest of her clothes, and his, so they were both fully naked. She didn't think about how she looked to him. She was drinking in how utterly magnificent he was. To her eyes he had the perfect male physique, and when he stretched out on the bed beside her, her fingers thrilled to the sensual pleasure of touching him, the tight musculature, the satin-smooth skin, the whole shape of him.

It was probably wrong to make compari-sons, but she couldn't help thinking he was more essentially masculine than Flynn, stronger, harder. Tony King…a king amongst men. She smiled at the thought and he smiled at her smile, lifting a hand to lightly trace the curve of her mouth with his index finger, mak-ing her lips tingle, just as he made her whole body tingle, though he could do that with only a look.

''Happier now?'' he asked, his eyes sim-mering with pleasure in her.

''Yes,'' she answered simply. It was true, though she didn't want to look at why. Maybe she was in shock at arriving where she now was. Maybe she'd moved beyond shock to a place where normal things didn't matter. Her mind whispered, *Let it be. Even if it was only for now, just let it be.*

His smile turned slightly crooked. "I hope we haven't committed a totally rash act. I didn't think about protection."

She frowned over the health concerns that hadn't even entered her head. It was an intrusion of a reality that jarred on her, yet ignoring it wasn't right, either. "You don't have to worry about me," she answered quickly. It was embarrassing to ask but a risk had been taken. She searched his eyes anxiously. "I trust you're…"

"In tiptop condition, yes. But there is the pregnancy issue."

A fast calculation relieved her on that score. "Safe," she assured him.

"You're on the pill?"

"No." At his raised eyebrows, she added, "No need. I haven't had sex for two years."

His brows dipped into a dark frown. "Two years," he muttered, as though that length of time seemed very unnatural to him.

She shrugged. "I haven't wanted to."

A sharp look. "But you wanted to with me?"

"Yes."

Eyes probing hers. "And you're happy about it?"

"Yes." For now, she was. How could she not be with a man like him wanting her like this?

His face cleared into a wide grin. "Well, so am I, Hannah O'Neill. Got to say you've had me in knots from the first moment of meeting."

"*You*...in knots?" She shook her head incredulously. "I thought you didn't like me."

"Didn't like the situation of an employee getting under my skin. It's a good rule...never mix business with pleasure."

Understanding clicked in. "I won't take advantage of this in our work situation, Tony."

"No, I don't believe you will." He stroked her cheek, his eyes adding their own warm caress. "It's very clear you're not a user, Hannah."

He wasn't, either. She was sure of it. He was a man who took control, who wore a mantle of responsibility easily, as though born to it. "A fair man," Megan had said, and Hannah didn't doubt it for a moment. Clearly he had guessed, known, felt that the physical attraction was mutual, which, of course, had triggered this outcome.

She thought what an extraordinary day it had been—this morning, fretting over the disturbing strength of Tony's sexual impact on her, finding how amazingly real it was this afternoon, and in between... Jodie and Flynn with all the blighting memories of their betrayal of her trust in so many things.

Tony saw the happy light in her eyes dim just before her lashes lowered, veiling the clear green windows to her soul. He instantly sensed she'd gone to that bleak place she didn't want to share with him. Had he said anything to lead her down that road?

Not a user...

But Jodie Lovett was.

And two years of celibacy, feeling no need for sex.

Maybe a woman could hold back physical frustration that long without feeling too much stress. Women were certainly different to men. Nevertheless, it smacked to Tony of a deliberate disassociation from her own sexuality, and that spelled big hurt. Not physical or she wouldn't have responded to him as she had. No, this was emotional trauma so deep it had turned her off getting close to a guy, probably in every sense, and from her reaction to Flynn Lovett...

Was she thinking of him?

Comparing?

Primitive instincts surged to the fore again, demanding action that would spin his rival right out of her thoughts.

"Unbraid your hair!"

*   *   *

The command jolted Hannah out of her bitter memories. She was with Tony…Tony who was looking at her with such fierce desire in his eyes she was instantly flooded with the heat of his focus on her and the energy behind it—such powerful energy, pouring into her heart, making it leap with excitement.

"My hair?" she repeated in mesmerised wonder that he did desire her so much.

"I'm into unknotting everything right now," he declared with a challenging little smile. "I want to see it flowing free."

Free… It was a magic word, dispelling all the emotional baggage that had weighed her down today. The idea of being completely free with Tony was exhilarating. She sat up to have both hands free to undo the band that kept the braid fastened, then pulled the thick rope of hair over her shoulder so she could see to unknot it.

Tony clamped his hands around her waist and with seemingly effortless ease, lifted her to straddle him as he rolled onto his back, settling her in very intimate contact right over the apex of his thighs, which he raised enough to hold her precisely in that provocative position, grinning wickedly as he said, ''I need you there so I can watch you properly.''

She couldn't help laughing. There was absolutely nothing *proper* about this. It was definitely wicked, deliciously wicked, and the wanton creature who had emerged in Hannah when Tony had taken hold of her on the balcony, stirred into life again, urging the fun of teasing, the satisfaction of exciting Tony, watching him watching her.

Just a slight undulation of her hips and his semi-aroused state showed immediate interest in the stimulation, coming to full attention so quickly, the stimulation became highly mutual and so tantalising, Hannah could barely keep her fingers working on loosening the thick swathes of her braid, especially when Tony started caressing her breasts, lightly fanning her nipples with his thumbs, a totally absorbed expression on his face, his eyes simmering their pleasure in every aspect of her body.

It made her feel incredibly sexy, even more so when she shook her hair loose and he wound long rippling waves of it around his hands and pulled her down to him, kissing her with wildly erotic passion as the mass of her hair tumbled around both their faces, increasing the sense of intimacy, of diving headlong into a secret world of their own—just Hannah and Tony.

''Put me inside you.''

Yes, she thought, yes...raising herself enough to do it, and even as she felt the exquisite sensation of him sliding into her, he was lifting her breasts to his mouth, taking them, drawing them in just as she was drawing him in, a deep, deep suction that tipped her into explosive action, wanting him to feel the same piercingly sweet sensations as strongly as she did...together...as one...more and more and more so...and the wild intensity of it glittered in their eyes, sharing the frenzy of feeling, exulting in it, loving it, loving each other for the sheer experience of it, driving it beyond all control to a climax so powerful, Hannah was a melting mass of quivering nerve-ends, awash in an ecstatic sea of sensory pleasure, and Tony was cradling her, stroking her, kissing her, making her feel she was wonderful and an endless delight to him, the wanting a continuous stream, not finished, not even diminished.

He was making love to her, she thought, and it didn't matter that they barely knew each other in any conventional sense. It felt so good…right…perfect…she didn't want to question it. Again her mind whispered, *Let it be, just let it be.*

All the conscious knowing she had believed in with Flynn hadn't proved true. All the planning she'd done towards their wedding… wasted in the worst possible way. Better to let life happen, not think too far ahead with this relationship. It would evolve into whatever it was meant to. Right now, all she wanted to think, to feel, was…Tony.

CHAPTER NINE

ISABELLA VALERI KING cast her eye around the grand ballroom, checking that all was as it should be for this wedding reception. King's Castle certainly provided a splendid venue for such happy functions and usually she took pleasure in seeing that everything was running perfectly, as it seemed to be this evening. However, the joy shining from the faces of the newly married couple at the bridal table was another reminder of Antonio's frustrating lack of co-operation in her plans for him.

She had specifically asked him to come by the castle this afternoon, ostensibly to reassure her she had chosen a good chef for *Duchess*— a perfectly reasonable request in the circumstances. Her main objective had been to gauge his interest in Hannah O'Neill, whether or not he had the good sense to see her as a possible partner for him in the journey of life.

They had definitely found each other attractive. Isabella had not missed the signs of a heightened physical awareness between them. *The chemistry,* as her very wise niece, Elizabeth, explained it, was there to draw them together. What Isabella wanted to know was what might keep them apart, and if she could play a hand in removing any problems.

She could do nothing without knowledge. Which made Antonio's failure to visit her, as he said he would, all the more vexing. On the other hand, it wasn't like him not to keep his word. Something must have prevented him from coming. Though he should have had the courtesy to call and let her know.

Feeling the need to talk over her discontent with Rosita, Isabella made a discreet departure from the ballroom, returning to the private quarters of the castle where she might make her own telephone call to her errant grandson.

Or one to Hannah O'Neill, inviting her to afternoon tea on her day off.

A glance at her watch showed seven-fifteen. She had eaten earlier, but undoubtedly she would find Rosita in the kitchen, still half expecting Antonio to show up and maybe want something to eat. For over twenty years Rosita had been spoiling Isabella's three grandsons. It was high time they were more considerate of the woman who had served them all so well.

She entered the kitchen in a disgruntled mood and came to a startled halt when Antonio himself entered in a rush by the other door which led through the utility room to the grounds surrounding the castle. He was in his captain's uniform, as though he'd just come from *Duchess,* and he headed straight for the wall telephone, tossing apologetic words at her without so much as a pause in his step.

"Sorry I'm late, Nonna. Something came up and it hasn't gone away. Got to make a call. Only be a minute or two. Hi, Rosita. And no,

I don't want anything to eat, thank you. I'll be dining out.''

He was dialling even as he spoke. Isabella held her tongue. Antonio was emanating urgency and the fire of determination was in his eyes. She'd seen that look on his face many times, from when he was only a boy. It meant he was going into battle and nothing was going to turn him away from it, regardless of the odds against him.

She glanced at Rosita who was sitting at the island bench, paused in her self-appointed task of making pastry for whatever she planned to cook tomorrow. They exchanged a worried look, both of them aware of how Antonio acted when he was all stirred up.

In his determination not to lose, he could be dangerously reckless, taking risks that a less competitive person would never take. He counted on his force of will to carry him through and mostly it did. But this trait in Antonio's character always struck fear in Isabella's heart.

"Nautilis?" he said into the receiver.

Isabella frowned. The Nautilis was a very high-class restaurant, where President Clinton himself had chosen to dine when he had visited Port Douglas—certainly not the place for a battle.

"It's Tony King. There was a couple on *Duchess* today, name of Lovett. First names Flynn and Jodie. They mentioned they'd booked a table with you tonight. Would you be able to check that for me, please?"

His tone was pitched to a matter-of-fact enquiry, not suggesting any unpleasantness—simply one local business asking a small favour of another local business.

"Thank you. What time are you expecting them?"

He checked his watch, nodding at the reply.

"I'd like to dine there myself tonight. Can you fit in another table for two? I realise this is late notice but I would appreciate it very much if..."

A grim look of satisfaction on his face indicated a positive reply. Isabella was anxiously wondering about the companion he intended to take with him. Was there some other woman entering the scene? Another one of his come-and-go relationships, wasting time and opportunity?

"Thank you. We'll be arriving at eight-thirty. One other favour... I'd rather not be placed on the same deck as the Lovetts' table. They caused me some trouble today..."

Trouble... So why go looking for more of it, Antonio? The restaurant had split-level dining areas but both levels were open to each other and all guests could be easily viewed.

"They're placed on the upper deck and you'll put us on the lower deck. Fine! Thank you very, very much."

He replaced the receiver, his eyes glittering with triumph at having successfully made the arrangements he wanted. The battle ground was set. But what were the issues at stake?

"Antonio..." Isabella started gravely.

He had the gall to grin at her. "Got to move it, Nonna. Shower, shave, change of clothes. I'll chat to you tomorrow. Promise."

"Two minutes," she demanded. "You can give me two minutes. You're not due at the restaurant for another hour and it doesn't take you that long to get ready to go out."

"Okay. What do you want to know in two minutes?"

He was tense underneath the token indulgence, wanting to go up to his room and get on with the plan he had in mind. He folded his arms with an air of patience, but Isabella read that piece of body language as sheer belligerence—nothing was going to stop him in any significant way.

"Hannah O'Neill," she said, and felt a spark of triumph herself when she saw his hands clench. He was certainly not indifferent to Hannah. Was the battle he intended to fight linked to her in some way? "Is she fitting in well?" Isabella pressed.

"Fine!" he answered tersely. "The crew like her. She can cook fish. I intend to keep her on. Satisfied?"

He started moving, assuming he'd said enough.

"I take it Hannah is still in the Coral King apartment Alessandro gave her?"

"Yes." He hesitated, frowning slightly. "Why do you ask? Monday is her first day off. She's too busy to look for a place before then."

"Oh, I was just thinking of giving her a friendly call. Now that you're finished with the telephone and too busy to chat with me yourself..."

"Don't!" The word was shot at her so fast it had the impact of a bullet being fired from a battle line.

Isabella drew herself up with straight-backed hauteur and gave him an arched look of reproof. "I beg your pardon?"

The aggression pumping from him was reined in. He made a curt, dismissive gesture, realising he had no authority whatsoever over her decisions or actions. ''Sorry, Nonna. I happen to have a situation with Hannah that needs careful handling. If you want to call her, please do it tomorrow, not tonight.''

''You just told me everything was fine with her.''

''It will be,'' he muttered darkly.

''But it isn't right now,'' Isabella claimed with utter certainty.

Another sharp, dismissive gesture. ''Hannah almost walked out of the job today because of a couple who came on board. She doesn't want to talk about the past history they've obviously shared but they're not letting go, Nonna. They want to get their hooks into her again and I'm not about to stand for that.''

''So…it's Hannah you're taking to the Nautilis tonight.''

''Yes.'' His eyes narrowed with ruthless intent. ''She needs to be free of that pair. One way or another I'm going to kill their games stone-dead.''

Violent feeling shimmered from him. Without a doubt he was deeply engaged with Hannah O'Neill. But was he getting it right for her?

''Antonio, does Hannah know what you plan?'' she asked pertinently.

''She'll be with me,'' he answered with such passionate emphasis Isabella knew instantly that Antonio was taking this fight into his own hands.

''You will throw her into the ring with these people she wishes to avoid?''

''You think running away solves anything, Nonna?'' he flared back at her. ''Two years she's been running from them and she would have run again if I hadn't acted fast this morning.''

Isabella shook her head, having sensed none of this fear in Hannah O'Neill. She had seemed such a happy person, happy, confident, carefree…

''Are you sure this is so, Antonio?''

He nodded grimly. "It stops tonight. Hannah will stay with me."

The possessive ring in his voice should have warmed Isabella's heart, giving her hope that Antonio had at last found a woman he might come to love and cherish, but again she was lacking knowledge, crucial knowledge.

"You are doing what you want. But is it what Hannah wants? You say she hasn't talked of this past. You are taking on an enemy without knowing what it is."

"They're like a cancer on her soul," he retorted vehemently. "That's enough reason for me to get her to face them and choose to be rid of them."

"Ask her, Antonio," she urged. "Ask her if this is what she wants."

"Stay out of it, Nonna," he warned. "Just stay out of it. It will be how I want it to be."

He strode off, not prepared to listen to reason.

"He wants to rescue her," Rosita said quietly.

"He might be telling himself that, Rosita, but he is acting like a bull who is blindly intent on driving off another bull."

"You mean he is protecting his territory."

Isabella heaved a sigh of exasperation. "This could go badly."

"You don't think Antonio will win?"

"What makes a woman run from a married couple? What if the cancer on Hannah O'Neill's soul is an unfulfilled love? A love that was forbidden to her?" She shook her head, wishing she knew more. "There is a reason why Hannah will not talk of these people."

"If the man is married, then he is no good to her," Rosita argued, picking up the roll of pastry, slamming it down on the marble square and kneading it with far more energy than she needed to.

Antonio's energy making her jumpy, Isabella thought. The power of it was still hanging around, making them both feel highly unsettled. "This Flynn Lovett cannot be happily married,'' she pointed out. ''Antonio sees him as a threat. A happily married man is no threat. If this man is considering a divorce...''

''Divorce is not good,'' Rosita declared firmly, giving the pastry a good punch. ''I think Antonio should save her from such bad things.''

Which was all very fine if she wanted to be saved, Isabella thought, but it was her experience that these days young women preferred to make their own independent choices.

Rosita was in her sixties and very Italian in her thinking. A man took care of such things. That was what a man was for—to fight for his woman and make the world a better place for her. A woman looked after the household and the children.

Isabella was wishing life could be that simple and people a lot less complicated when Rosita paused in her pummelling of the pastry and looked at her with all too knowing eyes. ''There is no stopping Antonio, Isabella. You know there isn't. What will be will be.''

This fatalistic view did not sit at all well. "He cannot make Hannah choose what he wants," she fretted. "It's all too fast. He should have moved her out of their way, taken the time to win her first. It's the wrong hand to play. He'll ruin everything."

"You thought Alessandro had ruined everything with Gina by acting too quickly," Rosita reminded her.

"Yes, but we knew Gina's background. We knew he could surmount her fears and objections."

"We know Hannah O'Neill's background, too. It is one of strong family. No divorce. That girl does not want a messy life. She ran away from it. Perhaps Antonio is right to make the stand and fight for her."

"It's a risk he didn't need to take."

"That is the man he is. If it is wrong for her, then *he* is wrong for her and they will not be happy together."

It was a line of logic Isabella could not refute.

Antonio was…Antonio. Totally elemental. No subtlety. All the polish she'd tried to give him…no more than a very thin veneer. His genes were probably a direct throwback to the genes from her husband, born and bred in the Outback, one of the Kings of the Kimberley.

Edward…

She remembered he'd taken one look at her—such a look it had made her toes curl—and said, "You are mine, Isabella Valeri."

And she was.

There had never been another man for her.

But that was sixty years ago and times had changed.

Whether Antonio was right or wrong for Hannah O'Neill…well, that was in the lap of the gods now.

CHAPTER TEN

TONY'S adrenaline was running high as he strode around the jeep to help Hannah out. She was wearing high-heels. Very sexy high-heels. Red, which looked great against her honey-tanned bare skin, with just thin little straps around her ankles and across her toes holding them onto her feet. She definitely needed help getting out and feeling steady in those shoes.

He opened the passenger door. Hannah swung her legs towards him. The filmy fabric of her dress slewed slightly, opening up the thigh-high side slit, semi-disguised by the soft ruffle that ran around the hem of the skirt. Very provocative, that ruffle. There was one around the V-neckline, too, forming filmy little sleeves over her shoulders and accentuating the soft swell of her cleavage. Fabulous dress, with big splashes of pink-red floppy poppies running down in a diagonal against a creamy background that was the exact same colour of some of the strands in her hair.

He loved her hair, rippling way out over her shoulders, a rioting mass of crinkly waves in an incredible array of blonde shades from cream to honey, all intermingled and looking great. It flowed towards him as she bent forward to stretch her legs down to the street. Shiny and soft from being freshly washed, it smelled of lemons, and he instantly thought how much he would enjoy burying his face in it later tonight.

She linked her arm around his, hugging it as she set her feet on the ground and straightened up. ''Thanks, Tony.'' A slightly rueful smile was flashed at him. ''I think I'll have to hang on to you. I haven't worn these shoes for a while.''

He laughed, brimming over with pleasure in her as he clamped his other hand over the one resting on his arm. ''When a man has a woman as beautiful as you are, hanging on his arm, he's not about to let her slip away. I want everyone to know you're mine, Hannah O'Neill.''

Her lovely green eyes danced pleasure right back at him. ''Well, I'm very happy to claim you as mine, too, Tony King.''

''Just keep holding that thought,'' he advised.

She laughed, not realising he was deadly serious.

As they set off on the walk to the restaurant, Tony had a few moments' trepidation about what he was leading her into. She was happy with him. Right now all the vibrations between them were positive. Should he take her elsewhere and build on that happiness, making it a platform that would seal off the past for her? Was that possible?

Even if it was, could he live with not knowing what her choice would have been if Flynn Lovett made himself available to her?

Winning by avoidance…

No. The choice to run was wrong. It might have been right for Hannah two years ago, but not now. Not with him. He had to know…and she had to know…just how much being with him counted. Talk meant nothing. Action and reaction showed the truth.

The Lovetts were staying in Port Douglas for another three days. They'd told him so. Better to force the connection between them and Hannah tonight and break it, once and for all. Bury it so it never raised its head again.

They reached the gate to the private path up to the restaurant. He paused, knowing once they were past this gate there'd be no turning back. Should he tell Hannah what she was about to face? His grandmother's voice echoed through his mind. *Ask her if this is what she wants.* But if she chose to run again…

No!

He couldn't bear for either Flynn or Jodie Lovett to have that much power over her.

She was his. She wanted to be with him. She

was hanging on to his arm and no one was going to come between them.

He opened the gate.

Hannah took a deep breath as Tony closed the gate behind them. Her whole body was buzzing with excitement. It was such a beautiful evening…the balmy atmosphere of this lovely laid-back tropical town making any sense of turmoil absurd, plus being with Tony, who not only made her *feel* beautiful, but was so beautiful himself, incredibly sexy and wanting to keep their pleasure in each other going, insisting she dine with him at this top-line restaurant.

It was lucky she had held on to this dress and the shoes that went with it so she had something decent to wear. More than decent. She'd thought it wonderfully feminine and glamorous when she'd seen it modelled during the last fashion week she'd done, and it had been a gift of appreciation from its designer for her work on the show—a reminder of her other life, but she'd never worn it for Flynn. He'd never even seen it. She'd been keeping it to…

She shook her head free of the memory. Tony was turning back to her, taking her arm again, and she was glad she still had the dress to wear for him, to mark this evening as very special, because it was. *He* was special. Amazingly so. And stunningly handsome in his red sports shirt and fawn chinos. Even the colours they were wearing more or less matched. It seemed to reinforce the sense of being a couple, boosting her spirits even higher.

She happily hugged his arm as they started up a path that revealed how very special the Nautilis restaurant was, too. They were instantly plunged into a mini-rainforest which completely shut out the town behind them. Ahead and above them, seemingly just hanging there amongst the trees and ferns and beneath a canopy of towering palms, were open wooden decks where people were seated in high-backed cane chairs, dining under the light of candles set in huge black wrought-iron candelabras.

"Oh, this is wonderful!" Hannah breathed, thinking it was the epitome of tropical romance, placing an oasis of sophistication in the heart of a primeval setting.

"They do a great dish with mud crab, too," Tony dryly informed her.

She laughed, her eyes mischievously teasing as she asked, "You think I should pick up some pointers from the cuisine? Is this why you brought me here?"

"No." There was a touch of wryness in his smile. "This has nothing to do with your culinary expertise."

Her stomach contracted as memories of their physical intimacy flooded through her. "Well, I'd have to admit I've never cooked mud crabs so maybe I can learn something," she rattled out, wondering if he meant to spend all night with her and admitting to herself she wanted him to.

"They are a specialty of far North Queensland."

"Then I *will* have to learn. I love this part of Australia."

"Enough to live here?"

Her heart skipped as she looked into eyes that seemed to be seriously questioning. Could he mean he wanted her to? That perhaps they might make a future together?

Surely it was far too soon for such questions.

"I don't know yet," she answered lightly, shying from the inner tension of putting too much on the line.

The path had led them to a flight of steps that zig-zagged up to the reception deck above the two dining levels. Tony gestured for her to go ahead of him. "Better hold the banister as you go up," he advised, releasing her arm so she could.

Feeling extremely conscious of Tony following her and needing to lessen her physical awareness of him, not wanting her legs to suddenly turn to jelly when she was wearing such precarious shoes, Hannah rushed into more speech as she mounted the steps.

"You know, I had two marvellous weeks at Cape Tribulation before coming on down to Port Douglas. Was the tea plantation I saw there the one your grandmother said you manage?"

"Yes, though I manage two," he answered matter-of-factly. "The biggest one is near Innisfail."

"Plus the Kingtripper Company." No wonder he flew a helicopter to keep in touch with all his business interests.

"The Kingtripper line is my personal baby. The tea plantations are part of the family holdings," he explained.

Born and bred to responsibility, she thought, and probably thrived on the challenge of taking on more. He certainly shouldered it with an ease attained by very few people. "Your family must carry a lot of weight in these parts,

Tony,'' she remarked. ''A long history here. Property...''

''What about your own family, Hannah?'' he inserted quietly.

''Oh, on the whole we're a productive lot. My father is an inventor. My mother is a writer. My brothers and sisters are all high achievers in one field or another.'' She slanted him a self-mocking little smile as they finally reached the top landing and he stepped up beside her. ''I'm the only drop-out.''

His eyebrows tilted. ''Any regrets?''

She shook her head. ''None.''

It was true. She didn't want to go back to the frantic pace of a life that was driven by the demands of tight deadlines. Too many pressures had contributed to her ignoring things she should never have ignored, and neglecting her own needs in favour of getting the job done. She would never let work dominate her life again, not to that extent anyway.

Feeling very content just to be here at this marvellous place, she smiled at the woman who came forward to greet them.

"Tony, lovely to see you here."

"Glad you could fit us in," he answered warmly.

"And this is…?"

"Hannah." Tony took her arm again, smiling an appeal at the other woman as he added, "Hannah O'Neill, wanting to sample your mud crab. Not all gone, I hope."

"You are late-comers," the woman warned. "I'll have a word in the kitchen after I see you to your table. Or would you like a drink at the bar first?" She gave Tony a look of knowing sympathy and nodded towards the dining deck just below them. "The other party is settled."

What other party? Hannah wondered.

"We'll order drinks from the table," Tony decided.

"Fine! Let's go then."

She led off to the steps which took them down to the first dining level. As they followed, Hannah was still wondering about *the other party*. Tony hadn't mentioned meeting someone else here but there must have been talk of it when he'd made the booking. A little disappointed that he had some secondary motive for bringing her to this place, not just a special night out for the two of them, she glanced around the seated diners to see if anyone was signalling their presence to Tony.

Her heart stopped dead.

So did her feet.

Flynn!

Flynn staring at her, rising from his chair.

"Hannah?" Tony's voice, his hand clamping over hers, demanding her attention. "Just watch the steps," he instructed. "I won't let you fall."

The steps.

She wrenched her gaze from the man she would have married and looked down, made her feet move forward. Tony was holding her. He would guard her from any approach from Flynn. He'd done so this afternoon and he would do it again now. She had to concentrate on not letting her legs wobble from the shock of seeing him here, seeing him looking at her as he used to, eating her up with his eyes as though…

No! She wasn't going to remember that. Too late. Too long gone. Too wrong. He'd made his bed with Jodie.

"I booked a table on the next deck down," Tony said, telling her they were not staying on the same dining level as Flynn.

Relief.

Moving on.

No one calling out her name.

Nor Tony's.

Another set of steps.

Then to a table for two in the far corner of the lower deck, as far away as it was possible to get from Flynn's table, although he could undoubtedly see her from where he was, watch her if he wanted to. But he couldn't see much because Tony settled her in the chair that faced away from Flynn and the solidly woven cane of the high back rest gave her a large measure of privacy. Since he wasn't in her line of sight at all, she could pretend he wasn't here, except she knew he was. And Jodie had to be with him. The two of them together.

She dimly heard Tony order some recommended cocktails and a bottle of wine. They were handed menus. On some automatic level Hannah smiled and nodded at whatever was said. She couldn't concentrate her mind on the printed menu. When suggestions were made, it was easier to agree to them. Food was no longer of any interest to her.

They were left alone.

She took a deep breath, trying to put Flynn and Jodie behind her in every sense, and looked directly at Tony, needing him to keep her distracted from the couple she didn't want to think about. Her heart contracted as the watchful intensity in his eyes sent another shock wave through her system.

He knew what she was feeling.

He knew Flynn and Jodie were here.

He had known all along.

They were *the other party!*

"Why?" she blurted out.

He didn't try to pretend ignorance. His eyes blazed with determined purpose, and she felt the steel will behind them, ready to undercut any protest she might make. His reply was as direct as her demand.

"Because I don't like what's going on between you and the Lovetts and it's time it stopped."

Her hands fluttered an agitated appeal. "You don't understand…"

"Then try making me understand, Hannah."

It wasn't a request. It was a command. A flat-out challenge that he was not about to let her back away from. He leaned forward, reached across the table and took her hand, transmitting the warmth and strength of his touch, forcefully reminding her of how much they had shared of themselves with each other.

"You're with me. You have been *very intimately* with me this afternoon. Yet now you are letting them intrude on us. You are letting them impinge on our time together. What gives them the power to do that, Hannah?''

He was right. It was wrong to blight her present with Tony with painful memories of people who had nothing to do with him.

''I'm sorry. It's just…I haven't seen them for two years and they bring back…what was.''

''So let's have *what was* out in the open so I know what I'm dealing with. You've held on to it too long. Share it with me.''

''I'd rather not. I'd truly rather not, Tony. I'm sorry I let them distract me. Please…let's talk of other things. Tell me about the tea plantations. Please? I want to know more about you.''

''And I want to know more about you. Why you run, Hannah. You dropped out and ran and you're still running. I don't want to be used as your escape route. And that's what you're doing right now.''

He paused to let that sink in, his eyes deriding any other interpretation of her response to the situation. Hannah see-sawed between shame and panic, knowing what he said was true, yet feeling sick at the thought of revealing the worst moments of her life when the bottom had dropped out of her world and everything had turned black. It was too humiliating to talk about.

"Be fair to me, Hannah."

His voice was softly urging but it was another command. He was dictating how their relationship should go. And as much as she recoiled from baring her soul, an inner voice whispered she had already bared her body to him and that had felt good…right. Shouldn't she try trusting him with more?

He had stood by her today.

He was standing by her now.

But she would lose him if she wasn't fair. That was what was on the line. And suddenly the way forward was very clear, dictated by one vital, overriding factor.

She didn't want to lose Tony King.

CHAPTER ELEVEN

EVERY nerve in Tony's body was piano-wire tight as he waited for Hannah's decision. Her gaze lingered on their linked hands for what felt like aeons. He wanted to increase the strength of his hold on her, make withdrawal impossible, but he knew physical force would not win what he needed from her. This battle was for her heart and mind and soul and she had to give them up to him willingly.

He didn't stop to think why it meant so much to him. It just did. And he knew he would refuse to accept failure. She had to realise what he'd said was true. She had to realise he was on her side and would fight whatever demons plagued her memory, rendering them completely powerless…if that was possible.

He'd seen Flynn Lovett stand as he caught sight of Hannah, seen the stunned surprise on his face turn to an unmistakable lust for the Hannah who was dressed so desirably tonight, seen Jodie Lovett pull him down again, and the flash of angry frustration he'd shot at his wife as he submitted to her anger at his reaction.

There was trouble brewing at that table and Hannah was the focus of it. Tony didn't want to believe Flynn Lovett still resided in her heart, didn't want to believe that she wouldn't—couldn't—give him up. He hoped it was no more than a deep scar that could be erased and she would let him help her get rid of it.

Try me, he willed at her with all the energy he could harness.

Trust me.

"All right," she murmured, lifting her lashes to show him eyes that swam with vulnerability, stopping any triumph he might have felt stone-dead.

This was a bad journey for her. He'd pressed her into it and now he had to ease the way as best he could. He lightly squeezed her hand, wanting to impart reassurance as he quietly said, "I'm a good listener, Hannah. Don't worry about what you're telling me. Just spill it out and I'll still be here at the end of it, still wanting to be with you. Okay?"

She managed a wry little smile. Her hand slid away from his as she sat back, visibly gathering herself to re-visit the past. Tony sat back, too, careful not to make her feel crowded by him. Their cocktails arrived, giving her more time to find a starting point. She seized on hers, eagerly sipping it as though her mouth was very dry. He waited, sure in his own mind she would not backtrack on her decision to open up to him. It was important to keep his own reactions under control now.

"I used to be part of a very high-level team that organised events," she began. "We took on festivals, exhibitions, big money functions, fashion shows. We created themes to match the mood or personality of the event, organised the lighting, the music, the props, the seating—'' a shrug ''—whatever was required for the outcome to have maximum impact. It was also our job to ensure everything ran as planned.''

''A lot of responsibility,'' Tony remarked encouragingly, thinking that making *an event* of presenting Matt's exotic tropical fruit was a piece of cake for someone with her background experience.

She nodded. ''And pressure. The pressure was always on to perform, to deliver what we promised. We put in long hours. Travelled at the drop of a hat. It was exhilarating when we pulled off something big, but it was also a huge energy drain. Work sucked up most of my life. Even when I wasn't actively on the job, there were parties related to work, people to meet, contacts to make.''

''The treadmill never stopped,'' Tony inserted, nodding his understanding.

A self-mocking smile tilted her mouth. ''More like a roller-coaster. *I* never stopped to look where I was going or ask myself why, or even whether it was truly what I wanted. I didn't learn to do that until after I dropped out.''

"Most people are carried along by the stream they're in, Hannah.''

She shook her head. ''That's no excuse for not making any effort to control it. Not choosing for myself.'' Her eyes dulled with painful reflection. ''For the last two frenetic years of my high-flying career, I even considered Jodie my best friend. Mostly because I shared an apartment with her and she was a constant in my life.''

They certainly weren't two of a kind, Tony thought.

''Actually, I was flattered that she asked me to share. Jodie is a few years older than I am and was—probably still is—a fashion buyer for a department store chain. Her flatmate had married and she was looking for someone who could afford half the rent on the apartment she'd leased at Bondi Beach. Very high-rental, very high-status place. I was earning big money and it was like another step up to me.''

Tony had little doubt Jodie Lovett would have manipulated that situation to her advantage. ''I guess you then found you had to fit in with her,'' he commented dryly.

Hannah looked surprised. ''Yes. She did want everything her way, but I didn't let it turn into open conflict because there were advantages to me, too. She used to get me fashion clothes on the cheap, and in lots of ways she was fun company, always full of in-crowd gossip. Our careers overlapped in areas like fashion week so we knew many of the same people.''

''And you would have extended her social network.''

''That went both ways. Jodie kept an A-list of eligible bachelors and used to wangle invitations to parties where they were likely to be. She dragged me along to them if she wanted a back-up woman in tow.''

''*Dragged* you?''

An ironic shrug. "More often than not I was too tired to enjoy them but Jodie would insist that I not miss *an opportunity*."

"But she was actually headhunting for herself."

Slowly, reluctantly, miserably, she conceded, "I think…the night I met Flynn…he was her target. Or maybe he became her target because he preferred me to her." She heaved a long ragged sigh. "I don't know. At the time she pretended she was happy for me, and she kept up that pretence right up to the week before our wedding."

Tony's stomach contracted at the shock punch of that information. She'd been on the verge of marrying the guy. Which had to mean she'd loved him. Might still love him. And Flynn Lovett sure as hell wasn't indifferent to her.

"I'd even chosen Jodie as my chief bridesmaid, ahead of my sisters," Hannah ran on. "She was involved in all the plans. You could say it was to be—" a sad grimace "—the biggest event of my life. I'd organised everything down to the last meticulous little detail.''

Her eyes glazed, her focus turned inward, and Tony knew she was envisaging how it would have been if the wedding had taken place—*the event* on which she would have brought all her expertise to bear to make it the most perfect, the most memorable, the most magical day of her life.

Over the years, his grandmother's involvement in weddings at the castle had demonstrated how much planning went into them to produce exactly the desired result on the day itself. More so when it was personal family, as with Alex and Gina. The whole build-up, the anticipation…he could imagine how totally shattering it would have been for it not to go ahead, to learn just a week before…

What?

What had been the irrevocable turning point?

And was it still irrevocable?

Her eyes flickered out of their glaze, pain sharpening their focus as she took a deep breath and said, "I trusted her. I trusted her to liaise with Flynn on the wedding plans when I was too tied up with work to get any time free. I thought she was my best friend."

Betrayal…deep and unequivocal.

Jodie had wanted Flynn and she'd got him, probably using every chance she had to set up meetings with him when Hannah was otherwise occupied. And Flynn had succumbed to temptation. Had he cursed himself for a fool ever since?

Their starters arrived—a selection of seafood with a hot salad, an easily consumed dish if Hannah's stomach wasn't in too much of a twist. Wine was poured from the bottle he'd ordered. Tony had finished his cocktail. Hannah was still sipping hers.

"Would you prefer water?" he asked, remembering her insistence on it this afternoon.

"I'm fine with this, thank you." Another wry smile. "I don't have to guard myself with you anymore, do I?"

"No. And I hope that feels good. It's a lonely business, guarding yourself. I don't want you to feel lonely with me." He smiled encouragingly. "Let's eat. You should never let anything spoil your pleasure in good food."

Her eyes crinkled with dry amusement. "It would be an insult to the chef not to try."

"Absolutely."

They ate. With how much enjoyment on Hannah's part, Tony wasn't sure, but she did eat everything and commented on the delicate flavour of the sauce, which meant she had focused on the food. He waited until their emptied plates were removed before leading her back to the critical mass in her mind.

"Tell me about Flynn, Hannah…what drew you to him, what drew him to you?"

She heaved a deep sigh and sat back again, eyeing him almost curiously, giving Tony the uncomfortable sense she was measuring his attraction against her experience with the man she'd planned to marry.

Flynn had lost her, he fiercely reminded himself.

He occupied the box seat now and he was not about to take any backward steps in the winning of Hannah O'Neill.

"I wasn't attracted to him at first," she said musingly. "Jodie pointed him out to me at the party and he certainly had a kind of commanding presence, but my initial impression was he was a bit too full of himself, and I didn't feel inclined to compete for his attention."

A blow to the ego of an A-list bachelor? Tony wondered cynically. A woman as beautiful as Hannah ignoring him?

"Why he chose to come after me, I don't know."

A challenge to be taken up and won, Tony thought.

"It was like he suddenly channelled all his energy into capturing my interest. It was very flattering and after a while, quite mesmerising. He was fascinating, very intelligent, witty, clever, and he exuded the kind of arrogant confidence that comes with knowing he dared more than most men and was on top of his game, which was trading commodities and manipulating international currencies. Somehow it gave him an exciting power.''

Her lashes lowered, veiling how much it had affected her. ''Anyhow, I fell for it.'' She took a deep breath and raised her gaze to his, her eyes hard with bitter mockery. ''I fell for the whole package. The black Porsche convertible, the apartment at Miller's Point with views of Sydney Harbour, the cupboards full of Armani suits, the glamorous courtship with champagne and roses and being whirled off to luxurious places. I loved it. I loved him. And when he asked me to marry him, I felt I was the luckiest woman in the whole world.''

A haunting disillusionment crept in as she added, ''And I believed he loved me. I never had any doubt about it. Not about anything. He said he liked the fact that I had such a full-on exciting career. It made me an extraordinary person to him, the kind of woman he wanted as his partner in life. There was never, never any criticism about the hours I had to put in. He worked long hours himself. I thought we were perfect for each other.''

''You didn't ever live with him?'' Tony asked, thinking that would have been a pertinent test of reality.

She shook her head. ''The question never came up. It wasn't as though we had a really long relationship. Only ten months in all. Short in today's terms.''

The length of time was irrelevant to Tony's mind. Impact could be immediate and lasting.

''So what happened a week before the wedding, Hannah?'' he asked softly.

Her head jerked in anguish. Then her chin set with the determination to finish it for him. The bleakness in her eyes echoed through her voice. ''I was bringing home my wedding dress. I'd had it made to my own design. I met up with my three sisters after work. They were picking up their bridesmaid dresses from the seamstress, too. I collected Jodie's as well as mine and invited my sisters back to the apartment to have a bit of a hens' night, spreading out the dresses, trying them on, making sure we all looked right. It was exciting…''

Her voice trailed off for a moment. Then she scooped in a deep breath and continued. ''My sisters were right on my heels when I reached the front door. We were all in high spirits, chatting, laughing. I guess I burst into the apartment and…'' She shuddered, reliving the shock, the horror of it draining her voice of any colour as she forced herself to go on. ''There they were, on the floor in the living room, in open view…''

''Jodie and Flynn.''

She nodded. ''Obviously, it had all been too urgent for them to make it to the bedroom, though there must have been some foreplay. Her blouse was hanging apart and…'' She swallowed convulsively. ''His trousers were down around his ankles…''

''Caught in the act,'' Tony murmured.

"And no…no hiding it…from any of us. I remember Jodie crying out that they couldn't help themselves. They were mad for each other and just couldn't help it. And Flynn blaming me, yelling if I hadn't been so caught up in my bloody work…and there I was, holding my wedding dress, with my sisters looking on. It was…unbearable. I threw the dress at Flynn and Jodie and bolted."

"Did he follow you?"

"Yes, but by that time I was back in my car. He tried to stop me from driving off. I think I would have run him over if he hadn't leapt out of the way."

"What about later?" The scene smacked of a deliberate set-up by Jodie, who must have known Hannah was due home with the dress.

"There was no later. I neither saw nor spoke to either of them again until today."

No real closure, Tony thought, and that was dangerous. If talking had been done then, she wouldn't be so much on edge now.

''I drove to my parents' home, told them the wedding was off, collected some clothes I'd stacked there, then kept on driving,'' she went on, her voice gathering the same grim, shut-out purpose that had been activated this morning. ''The next day I made the calls I had to make to cancel the wedding, assure my family I was okay, resign from my job which was no great drama since I'd been about to take time off for my honeymoon anyway. I simply... dropped out of the whole scene and left Jodie and Flynn to it.''

It wasn't simple. It was trauma on an extreme level—a double betrayal completely blowing her mind and everything else it had touched and tainted. She had survived it in her own fashion and Tony admired the way she had gradually restructured her life along different lines. No regrets about it, either. But the clean slate had ghosts that had never been confronted nor exorcised...ghosts that had to be dealt with and banished.

Nothing was ever totally black and white and Tony suspected it was the greys that haunted her, the greys that had never been allowed a voice. They had to be talked about. He had to know how much power Flynn Lovett still held over her heart, and it was better she face it now with him than continue to repress it.

"If Flynn begged your forgiveness, begged for another chance, could you love him again, Hannah?"

"No!" Sharp and emphatic, her eyes flashing instant recoil from the idea.

"You don't feel...he might have been entrapped by Jodie?" Tony probed carefully.

"Oh, I'm sure Jodie would have played her cards artfully but Flynn chose to pick them up," came the bitter truth. "He may well have enjoyed the kick of daring to, right under my nose." Her chin lifted in determined rejection. "I would never be able to trust either of them again."

"So you wouldn't accept any excuse."

"Would you, given the same circumstances?" she flared at him. "Would you forgive and forget, Tony?"

Anger...from deeply wounded pride. But pride could be a shield for far deeper feelings.

"I can't imagine myself doing so, no," he answered truthfully. "But I know from observing other people's relationships that the heart does find ways of accepting the unacceptable, especially if the offender is very persuasive and the injured party is still vulnerable to the love that was given. Infidelities do get forgiven, Hannah, even though they may not be forgotten."

A tide of heat washed up her neck and burned into her cheeks, making the flare of pride in her eyes very green. "I guess I'm no good at swallowing humiliation."

Humiliation beyond bearing...and nothing done—nothing allowed to be done—to alleviate it by the parties who had inflicted it, so it was still as strong as it had ever been.

Tony nodded, fully understanding now why she had wanted to walk off *Duchess* this morning and not have any contact whatsoever with the Lovetts. But by Hannah's extreme action of *dropping out,* both Jodie and Flynn had been robbed of any real closure with her, as well. That left the wound still tantalisingly, tormentingly *open,* perhaps more so to them than it was to Hannah—a running sore in their marriage.

Flynn might not have any chance with her but he was arrogant enough to give it a try, and if he was prepared to humble himself enough…would Hannah's pride crack?

Jodie would certainly do whatever she thought would queer Flynn's pitch.

The Lovetts had three more days in Port Douglas…time enough to find an opportunity to tackle Hannah on her own…unless they were stopped in their tracks tonight.

"Well, I'm sure this will be much sweeter to swallow," he said, smiling to lighten the mood as their waitress delivered the mud crabs to their table.

The business of serving gave Hannah time to recover some equanimity after the stress of her revelations.

"Enjoy," the waitress said as she left them.

"We will," Tony answered, shooting an appealing look at Hannah. "Let me get this straight now. You want Jodie and Flynn to go away and stay away. You want nothing more to do with either of them, regardless of how they might explain their actions, regardless of any appeal for your forgiveness or understanding. Is that where you stand, Hannah?"

"Yes." Her face was still flushed, eyes feverishly bright. "Do you think that's too mean of me, Tony?"

"No. It would be better, for your own sake, if you could feel indifferent to them, and I hope that will happen in time, but since I now understand where you're coming from, I'll simply get rid of them for you."

"Get rid of them?"

He grinned at her shock. "There used to be an Italian Mafia operating up here, extorting money from all the canefarmers. It was called *The Black Hand*. They cut off people's ears and hands…"

"Tony…" she pleaded frantically.

He laughed. "Relax. I was only teasing. My great-grandfather assisted in driving out *The Black Hand* decades ago. My family has always stood up to help people who couldn't find help anywhere else, Hannah."

Her tension eased. Her eyes softened. "That's a fine family tradition, Tony."

"Imbued in us from the old pioneering days. You have to look after your own. Which also covers feeding them. So please taste the mud crab. It's delicious."

She laughed.

It might only be from nervous relief but it sounded good to Tony. The weight on his heart lifted. He'd get her over this hump with the Lovetts. He wanted to hear much more of her laughter. He wanted to see her face light up for him and know the shadows of her past were completely gone.

Before they left this restaurant, Hannah O'Neill would be his.

That was the hand he intended to play.

CHAPTER TWELVE

AMAZINGLY, Hannah did enjoy the mud crab. Her stomach had stopped churning once Tony had teased her into laughing. The dreadful tightness in her chest had eased, too, and she found herself wanting to please him, to share his pleasure in the gourmet dish he'd ordered for both of them.

Somehow his sympathetic interest and calmly considered comments had drained away the angst of telling him about Jodie and Flynn. Or talking the whole miserable story through had unloaded the burden of all the bad feelings their presence here had stirred up again.

Tony was probably right in his judgement that keeping those memories bottled up gave them a power they shouldn't have any more. In any event, she was glad now she had shared them with him. And it was very heart-warming that he wanted to help her, though how he intended *to get rid of* Flynn and Jodie was a tantalising question.

He could hardly hound a couple of tourists out of Port Douglas…could he? How much influence did the King family have in this town? Clearly they had a long history here, and Tony had pressed to have this table tonight, precisely as he wanted it. That kind of manipulation made her feel uneasy. On the other hand, Flynn and Jodie had hardly been fair to her.

It suddenly struck her that what Jodie had said might have been true—that she and Flynn had been mad for each other and couldn't help themselves. Hadn't it been like that with Tony and herself this afternoon? What if they had fought against it, trying to be fair to her, and then with the wedding so close…

It might have happened that way. Though it seemed highly dishonest to her. How could a wildly strong mutual attraction be denied for so long? She looked at Tony and the desire that had swamped her earlier was instantly re-kindled. He really was the perfect man; beau-tiful, strong, kind, caring...*the white knight.* And very, very sexy.

He caught her look and his eyes zapped de-sire straight back at her, an electric current that linked them to the exclusion of everyone else. "Hello again," he said with a slow sensual smile that warmed her all over.

"Hello to you, too. I'm sorry for being dis-tracted from us. Will you tell me about the tea plantations now?"

He laughed and she thought how brilliantly handsome he was with his face lit up with pleasure. "Better if I show you, Hannah," he said, his eyes sparkling with happy anticipa-tion. "Come fly with me up to Cape Tribulation on Monday morning. I'll give you a tour."

"Fly? In your helicopter?"

"Quickest way to get there. Then on Tuesday we can fly to Innisfail and you'll see the whole picture."

"I'd love to do that, but have you forgotten? Mondays and Tuesdays are my only days off and I should look for a place of my own, Tony."

He waved dismissively. "That can wait. The apartment you're using isn't required for anyone else right now."

"But..."

"I'll square it with my brother and my grandmother. Okay?"

"No. I won't feel right about it. It's like...like sponging on your generosity. I can afford to be independent."

"Fine! Then this week you can pay Alex the rental you've figured out you can afford, and I'll explain to him it's my fault you haven't moved out yet because I took up your free days. How's that?"

She sighed, feeling she was being bulldozed but immensely tempted to give in to his persuasion. It was an exciting prospect, flying with Tony to whatever he wanted to share with her. "You're sure your family won't think badly of me?"

"Definitely not." He grinned. "Any thinking they might do will be centred on me. My grandmother will say…" He gestured exasperation and mimicked her voice, "Antonio…always in a rush. He cannot wait for anything."

Hannah couldn't help laughing.

"And Alex will say…" A roll of the eyes. "…A waste of time and breath arguing with Tony. He's like a bull at a gate."

"Are you?"

"Depends on the gate."

"And what will Matt say?" she asked, amused by this insight into their family relationships.

"Ha! That upstart brother of mine, trying to steal you right under my nose…" A dark lowering of his brows. "Matt will loudly complain that I'm deliberately taking up all your free time so he can't get a chance with you."

"And would that be true?"

The eyebrows lifted. ''Does he have a chance with you?''

''No.''

He grinned, a triumphant delight dancing in his eyes. ''Then we have nothing to worry about, do we? You'll come with me.''

Hannah's resistance to the plan melted away. Nothing to worry about was a wonderful state of mind. She wanted to have it. And she suddenly realised Tony was giving it to her, taking her out of Port Douglas on her days off so there could be no chance of further contact with Jodie and Flynn. This was his way of *getting rid of them,* as well as giving her something positive to occupy her mind.

She smiled at him, the smile going right down to her heart with this understanding of how he was taking care of her. Tony King…truly a king compared to all the other men she had known. ''Thank you, Tony,'' she said warmly.

Their waitress arrived to clear the table and take their orders for sweets. Hannah read down the selections on the menu, for the first time tonight actively interested in what was being offered. Having made her decision, she looked at Tony to query what he fancied. His gaze was not trained on the menu. His attention was intensely engaged by something on the upper dining level.

Hannah instantly tensed.

He was watching Jodie and Flynn. She didn't have to look to know that. The direction of his gaze, the hard set of his face, the sudden tautness of his body emanating a readiness to tackle trouble head-on.

"Tony?" The appeal spilled from her lips, anxiety surging at the prospect of being confronted by them again. They had married. Why couldn't they just get on with it and leave her alone?

"Ah!" His head swung to face her, the hardness wiped out by a quick smile. "Made your decision?"

"I thought...the soufflé..."

"Two," he said to the waitress, handing up his copy of the menu.

Hannah's was collected and the waitress departed.

"We're about to have company," Tony announced, his smile turning sardonic, his eyes glittering a challenge he expected her to meet. "Are you with me, Hannah?" The words transmitted strong vibrations of feeling that demanded a positive response.

"Yes," she forced from a throat that was choking up.

"Then show Flynn Lovett you are, very much so, by putting on a happy face and agreeing with everything I say."

"Just...Flynn?"

"Jodie left their table a couple of minutes ago. She walked off in high dudgeon, probably expecting him to follow. Flynn has not followed. On the contrary, he is now making his way towards us and I have no doubt his destination is this table. Now give me your hand and smile."

His hand was already reaching out. She met it without hesitation, wanting the physical connection with Tony and also needing to show Flynn she was now attached to a man who could not only match him in strong self-assurance, but beat him hands-down in the qualities that mattered more to her than material possessions and successes in the paper world of money markets.

There was a solidity to Tony King that Flynn would never have. She was proud to be with him—fiercely proud—and if there was any humiliation to be felt at this meeting, it would be Flynn's, not hers. She would not let him get to her.

"I won't let you down, Tony," she promised, gritting her teeth into a very determined smile.

"You will have to look at him, Hannah," he warned. "Treat him as you would any old acquaintance who's just passing by and stopping to say hello. Can you do that?"

Her nerves quivered at the pressure to perform as Tony wanted. His eyes blazed into hers, commanding her assent. She nodded, not knowing if she could deliver a semblance of social politeness but resolving to do her best.

"Mostly, you can look besottedly at me," he instructed, and grinned to make it easy for her.

Even so her heart skittered nervously as Flynn made a very aggressive arrival, drawing a chair from the vacated table next to them and placing it at theirs with the clear intention of seating himself with them. "Sorry to interrupt your twosome, but I'll only take up a few minutes," he tossed out, arrogantly assuming that neither of them would want to make a public scene by forcibly ejecting him from their company once he sat down, which he promptly did.

"You're not welcome, Flynn," Tony stated bluntly. "This is a very special night for us and you're intruding."

"Well, I'm sure you feel any night with Hannah is special, Tony. I certainly did," he claimed in a tone that raised Hannah's hackles so fast she had no problem at all in facing him with a look of arch surprise.

"Don't you think that line is a bit *off,* Flynn?"

His gaze locked onto hers, his brilliant brown eyes shooting their magnetism straight at her. "I self-destructed with you and have regretted it ever since. To me you were and always will be uniquely special, Hannah. I want you to know that."

Ashes…and strangely enough they weren't even bitter ashes. Not with Tony holding her hand. "It's a waste of time having regrets, Flynn," she said with a dismissive shrug. "You're married to Jodie…"

"We're getting a divorce."

"And Hannah is marrying me," Tony declared, shattering Flynn's shock announcement with his own and snapping their heads towards him.

"What?" shot out of Flynn's mouth.

It almost shot out of Hannah's mouth, as well. Her hand started to jerk up in a startled reaction, hitting against Tony's hold on it. He swiftly tightened his grip, squeezing to warn her off any further show of agitation, while smiling so besottedly at her, her heart did the startled leaping.

"This is the woman I love and will love till my dying day," he further declared. "And the miracle is, she feels the same way about me."

His tone of voice, the look in his eyes...it was so convincing Hannah's skin tingled all over.

"So you see, Flynn, your presence here is quite hopelessly out of place," he ran on, not bothering to even glance at the man who had tried to come between them. "We're not interested in your feelings. We're not interested in your marital problems. We're here, planning a future together, aren't we, Hannah?"

Another squeeze of her hand. "Yes. Yes, we are," she responded, smiling back at him in the same besotted fashion with no effort at all.

"Hannah…" It was a cry of exasperation, protesting the situation.

"Go away, Flynn," she said dreamily, still looking into Tony's eyes. "Your time was up a long time ago."

Which was the absolute truth! And it felt really really good to be able to say it with no angst whatsoever.

"Yes. Go away, Flynn. You are distinctly *de trop*," Tony said, his gaze locked on Hannah's as he lifted her hand to his mouth and grazed his lips warmly over her knuckles. "Would you like an emerald ring to match your eyes, my darling?"

"You'll waste your life in this hick town, Hannah," Flynn jeered, rising to his feet.

She ignored him. In fact, she took immense satisfaction in ignoring him. He deserved it for so rudely trying to cut out Tony who was definitely worth ten of him. More. Flynn wasn't even in the same category as Tony King.

Steaming with frustration, he virtually flung the chair he'd collected back to where it belonged and strode off.

"If that bastard gave you an emerald, I'll have to get you something else," Tony said mock seriously.

"No, it was a diamond. An emerald would be all yours," she informed him in the same vein.

His eyes grew properly serious. "You are well rid of him, Hannah."

"I know. And thank you very, very much for helping me. I don't know how you thought up that marriage line so fast but it sure was effective in cutting Flynn dead." She shook her head admiringly. "I almost died myself."

"You recovered superbly."

"You made it easy for me."

"It *was* easy." He cocked his head to one side assessingly. "And what does that say about us, Hannah?"

Her heart skittered. He couldn't mean...he wasn't really applying the idea of marriage to them. She shied away from any thought of rushing into a commitment. Having been so sure of Flynn...even though Tony was different…she instinctively recoiled from counting too much on a relationship, especially one that had barely begun. It was a big mistake to fall into fantasy. But what was *real* right now could be acknowledged.

"I think what it says about us, is that there are moments when we're very closely attuned to each other."

He nodded, seeming to weigh up her answer against some measure he had in his mind. Feeling she had short-changed him, and highly aware of how much he had come to her rescue, she fervently added, "And I also think you're quite wonderful, Tony King."

It sparked a wicked look. "Well, the night is young and I think you're quite wonderful, too, Hannah O'Neill. Can I take it that the past is past and the future is ours to make of it whatever we want?"

"Mmm…if that means I still get to fly with you," she answered lightly.

He laughed and kissed her hand again. "It certainly does. I fancy we may do quite a lot of flying together."

She heaved a happy sigh. What either of them would make of the future—together or apart—she had no idea. For so long now she had taken one day at a time, never planning too far ahead because then you started counting on the plans and they could go badly astray. It was better to simply take life as it came and hug all the spontaneous joys it brought.

Joy was bubbling up in her right now.

The night was young.

And she was with Tony King.

CHAPTER THIRTEEN

TONY had the emerald ring in his pocket. It was burning a hole in his pocket. He wanted it on Hannah's finger. The big question was whether she would accept it and she'd given him no solid encouragement to believe she would.

Yet she *was* happy with him. He was certain in his own mind that she loved him. It couldn't be otherwise. In the month since he'd got rid of Flynn Lovett they had spent all their spare time together and every minute of it had proved his instincts right. Hannah O'Neill was the woman for him in every sense and on every level. And he was right for her. He knew it in his bones.

So it was highly frustrating the way she shied from any talk of marriage. Just the mention of it and her gaze would slide away from his and she'd quickly fasten on some other line of conversation that led away from any talk of *the future*. It was almost as though she didn't want to think in any terms of permanence.

A butterfly…

Tony was beginning to feel haunted by the tattoo that just might symbolise Hannah's attitude to life, taking pleasure in a place and its people for a while, then flitting on. Was he simply part of her sojourn in Port Douglas? When it came to the end of the tourist season, did she intend to kiss him goodbye and move on?

She had her own apartment now, clearly determined on maintaining an independent situation, and she was always careful not to take any advantage of their intimacy on board *Duchess*. The chef was the chef and she did the job with such good cheer and appealing flair, the crew and passengers invariably responded positively to her. No one could ever say she hadn't given value in the position she held.

But was she really content, just being a chef? It hardly stretched the skills he knew she had. And while this part of far North Queensland was and always would be his home, she might come to view Port Douglas as *a hick town,* and start hankering for a more sophisticated city life again. Like Chris's partner, Johnny, who'd been happy enough to while away a year up here. But only a year.

He wanted to give her the ring. He wanted her to want what it symbolised. Impatience surged through him as he landed the helicopter in the castle grounds. Pressure of business had forced him to stay in Innisfail last night but today was Saturday, and a whole weekend with Hannah lay ahead of him—time to settle his doubts.

Regardless of any evasive tactic she tried to use he was going to propose marriage. What was the point of waiting any longer? The need to know where he stood with her was eating at him. Maybe he was being like a bull at a gate, but he'd either open the gate this week-end or smash it down.

He drove his jeep down to the marina in a very determined frame of mind. *Duchess* had been chartered for a family party today, only twenty-four passengers, so he might be able to snatch some private time with Hannah while they were anchored at the reef. One way or another, he had to pin down how she was thinking.

"So, how's it going with Tony?"

Hannah threw a startled glance at Megan. They were putting the salads away in the galley and such a direct personal question from her younger work-mate caught her by surprise.

Megan laughed. "We all *know,* Hannah. Just because you don't talk about it or throw it in our faces, you can't hide the vibes between you two. We're betting that Tony's down for the count this time."

"The count?" Hannah echoed.

"Fallen hard." A waggle of eyebrows emphasised the point. "And since you light up like a Christmas tree every time he's around..."

"Do I?"

"All smiles and sparkles. Gotta be love, I've decided."

"Well, since you're the expert," Hannah drawled teasingly. "Is it the great-while-it-lasts kind of love or the forever kind?"

"You mean...is Tony likely to walk you down the aisle?"

Hannah sighed. "Marriage isn't really the question. Divorce is so very common these days." Flynn and Jodie hadn't even lasted two years, and before that, Flynn hadn't lasted ten months before being unfaithful.

"Well, I can tell you one thing," Megan said, nodding seriously. "When the King family makes a commitment, it's rock-solid, providing you keep your side of the bargain. They're renowned for it. If any agreement with them falls through, you can be dead certain it's the other party who's broken trust. That's how they operate. So if Tony King asked you to marry him, he'd mean to make it work, Hannah. And he sure wouldn't like it if you were thinking of divorce as an option.''

''How do you know this, Megan?''

She shrugged. ''Lived here all my life. The Kings are like legends all up and down the far north. They go way back, you know? There are so many stories about that family standing by its word, playing fair, making things stick…that's just the way they are. Everybody knows that.''

Megan had said something about Tony being a very fair boss the day Jodie and Flynn had come on board *Duchess,* and he'd certainly made getting rid of them stick. As for standing by his word, he certainly hadn't let her down on anything yet, but it was still early days. The problem was, it was so easy to be in love with him, she couldn't quite bring herself to believe something so easy and wonderful would last. Just seeing him made her bubble with joy...but bubbles did break.

"Good morning!"

They both swung to face Tony who had just stepped into the saloon, bringing with him his own special charge of energy that instantly set Hannah's pulse racing and made her feel vibrantly alive.

"Morning!" Megan chimed back at him.

"Hi!" Hannah breathed, her mouth already breaking into a smile that precluded forming more words.

His smile, as always, illuminated how very handsome he was, and again Hannah could hardly believe her luck that he found her so attractive and their desire for each other was so blissfully mutual. At least her work couldn't come between them, she thought, happy to hold a relatively simple job that left her with plenty of hours for them to be together.

"The family party is streaming down the wharf now," he informed them. "I've forgotten their name."

''Anderson,'' Hannah replied.

''Is it some celebration? Birthday? Anniversary?''

''Family reunion.''

''Then they should be happy just talking to each other,'' he said with satisfaction, his eyes simmering with some private intent that definitely included Hannah.

The sound of voices moved him into his usual position to greet the incoming passengers who were always directed into the saloon by the dive team inviting them to get their coffee or tea and meet the captain.

Hannah quickly carried two cups to the coffee machine, ready for the first requests. She heard Tony say, ''Ah! Mr and Mrs Anderson, welcome aboard *Duchess*. I'm Tony King, your…''

''So you're Tony King,'' a voice she instantly recognised cut into Tony's spiel.

Shock speared through her. It was lucky she'd just put the cups down or they probably would have dropped from her hands. She stared disbelievingly at *her parents* who were eyeing Tony up and down as though they wanted to take in and assess every detail of his appearance and character.

"Yes, I am," Tony confirmed, looking somewhat perplexed at being the focus of such pointed interest.

"The man who's going to marry my daughter," her father ran on in his booming voice, galvanising stunned attention even from Megan.

"What?" spilled from her lips.

Hannah was speechless.

"I beg your pardon?" Tony queried, heavily frowning, as well he might, being faced with such an outrageous assumption.

"The name is not Anderson. It's O'Neill," her father corrected. "Connor O'Neill. My accountant booked the charter for me."

"O'Neill," Tony repeated dazedly.

"Hannah's father," came the pointed assertion. "This is her mother, Maureen. And may I say right here and now, we are not about to let you marry our daughter without her entire family present and we've come to make that known. Do I have your hand on that, Tony King?''

A hand was aggressively offered for Tony to take and shake on this man-to-man agreement. He shot a piercing look at Hannah, loaded with questions she couldn't answer. She was still speechless. Her stunned mind couldn't find any clue to how her father—her family—had arrived at the idea that she and Tony were getting married. It hadn't come from her. She hadn't even mentioned Tony to them in her e-mails. Not one word about their relationship.

A flood of heat rushed up her neck and scorched her cheeks. This was so embarrassing! He had to be thinking she had, at the very least, speculated to her parents about marrying him. His eyes glittered, undoubtedly from the electric activity in his mind. Then, apparently deciding the only way to rescue the situation and save her and her family major embarrassment, he seized her father's hand, pumping it vigorously and said what her father wanted to hear.

''You certainly have my agreement on that, Mr O'Neill. And may I say I'm delighted to meet you and Mrs O'Neill. I look forward to getting acquainted with the rest of Hannah's family today.''

A masterly piece of diplomacy. Hannah didn't know if she appreciated it or not. Didn't it perpetuate a terrible mistake which should be corrected?

Her mother then grabbed his hand with both of hers, pressing anxiously. ''You mustn't let Hannah talk you into some quick little register office wedding, Tony. I may call you Tony?''

''Of course.''

''I told her father we had to get up here in time to stop that. Thank God we could get this trip arranged before the month was up.''

''The month?'' Tony queried.

It completely blew Hannah's mind. They'd been worrying about a marriage between her and Tony for a whole month? She'd barely been with him that long! Only since the day Jodie and Flynn...understanding crashed through her confusion like a thunderclap.

"You can't get married under a month without a special licence," her mother rattled on. "Which was a worry, knowing how good Hannah is at organising things, but I hoped..."

"Mrs O'Neill..."

"You can call me Maureen, dear." Patting his hand in approval now.

Hannah opened her mouth to rush out an explanation for the situation that had brewed up because of Tony's tactic for getting rid of Flynn. Before she could manage to form sensible words, he plunged on, compounding the whole problem a thousandfold.

"Maureen, I can assure you Hannah and I will have a very proper wedding with all the trimmings and all family present. My grandmother would never speak to me again if we did anything else."

Hannah choked. It was one diplomatic step too far, letting her parents think there would be a wedding. She had to stop this. But how was it to be done without making Tony feel like a fool for coming to her rescue so gallantly in front of her parents?

Weddings could be cancelled, she thought wildly.

Who knew that better than she did?

"How long will you be staying in Port Douglas?" Tony went on charmingly, probably wondering how long he had to keep up the pretence. "I know my grandmother would love to meet you."

No, no, no! screamed through Hannah's mind. Isabella King might think it was real. They had to contain the damage, not spread it.

"Only the weekend," her father answered, much to Hannah's relief. She and Tony worked Sundays so...

"In that case, I'll re-arrange the crew roster for tomorrow so Hannah and I are free to be with you,'' Tony declared, ruining everything again.

Her mother beamed at him. ''That will be wonderful! I can see why Hannah…''

''Mum!'' Enough was enough! ''You, too, Dad!''

That snapped their attention away from Tony and their faces lit up with triumphant delight at sight of her behind the galley counter. Hannah still gave them both barrels of her displeasure at their gross assumptions.

''What on earth do you think you're doing, dragging the whole family up here and ex-pecting…''

''If Mohammed won't come to the moun-tain…'' her father rolled out.

Her mother hastily broke in. ''Hannah, we waited and waited for you to tell us about Tony yourself, and when you didn't…''

''I've got a right to my own private life!'' Hannah hurled at them.

''Now that's enough, young lady,'' her fa-ther boomed, marching up to the galley counter to dress her down. He was a big barrel-chested man who made a habit of mowing down any opposition and he went straight into attack mode, wagging his finger at her.

"We respected your need to flit off and find some new direction for yourself, never mind how much your mother worried about you. For two years you've deserted your family." His fist slammed onto the counter for emphasis. "Two years!"

"I kept in touch," she fiercely retorted, her eyes every bit as battle-green as his as they locked in challenge. "You always knew where I was and what I was doing."

"Travelogue stuff!" her father scoffed.

"Connor, stop scolding!" her mother cried, ranging up beside him, her slender build and the rather scatty mop of grey curls that framed a face full of friendly appeal belying the strength she wielded in the O'Neill household. "We're here to build bridges and don't you forget it."

Behind them, Hannah's sisters and brothers were spilling into the saloon, introducing themselves to Tony, closely followed by wives, partners, children, all creating a distracting hub-bub as they made happy comments about the forthcoming mythical marriage. The whole scene was hopelessly out of control, absolute chaos and getting worse by the second.

"Please don't be angry with us, Hannah," her mother was pleading.

"Maureen, she has no reason to be angry with us," her father instantly argued.

"I'm not angry," Hannah put in helplessly. "Just...surprised."

"Of course you are!" her mother agreed indulgently. "That was what it was meant to be. A lovely surprise!"

Twenty-four O'Neills descending on her—the whole family pressure-pack—with Tony haplessly cornered by their belief in a marriage that hadn't really been proposed or accepted. And she could see he was actually beginning

to enjoy the act, egged on by her rather bois-
terous family. She hoped he realised this was
all his own fault, using the getting-married line
to torpedo Flynn's arrogant attempt to chat her
up again.

"He's certainly a fine figure of a man,
Hannah," her mother said admiringly.

"I like him much better than Flynn already," her father declared, intent on mending
fences.

"Connor, we are not going to mention
Flynn," her mother chided.

"And why not when *he's* to blame for
Hannah playing this secret hand?" he growled.
"Here she is, too uptight to tell us anything in
case something goes wrong this time."

"That's not true, Dad." Hannah took a deep
breath, feeling more and more wrong about letting this deception run on. Tony didn't have to
save her face in front of her family. As for
bringing his grandmother into it, that was just
way over the top. Her family would simply
have to understand that their information had

been deliberately planted on a person who wasn't supposed to be in contact with them. Which reminded her... "Who told you about this?" she demanded.

Her mother grimaced apologetically as she replied, "Our Trish ran into Jodie Lovett at a fashion parade three weeks ago. Jodie made some catty remark about you and Tony King and your sister promptly dug her heels in and wouldn't let Jodie go until she had explained herself..." Her eyes telegraphed knowledge of highly suggestive intimacy as she added, "...very fully."

Hannah flushed, recalling that Jodie had seen Tony enter the Coral King apartment with her, as well as being witness to the dinner for two at Nautilis. No doubt Jodie had painted a vivid picture, and Trish, eager to believe her jilted sister did have a new fiancé, had probably elaborated on it to the rest of the family.

She could see them all speculating like crazy, especially when there had been no news from her about an engagement. Tony had never encountered the O'Neill clannishness—the networking that never stopped. It was one of the reasons Hannah had run two years ago. She couldn't have stood their overwhelming sympathy and caring, endlessly turning the knife in the wound of what had happened in their attempts to cosset and comfort.

''So when do you and Tony plan to marry?'' her father demanded to know.

''Dad...'' She heaved a sigh and gathered herself to lay out the truth. ''...we haven't even...''

''The ring!'' Trish called out excitedly, breaking from the pack around Tony, the lovely auburn hair she'd inherited from their father—although his was now white—being flipped over her shoulder as she rushed forward, completely forgetting the sinuous grace she used on the catwalk as a top-line model. ''Show us the ring, Hannah!''

It was the last straw of this whole ridiculous mess! Hannah glared at her busybody younger sister, opened her mouth and began to say, ''I haven't got...''

''She hasn't got it on,'' Tony loudly over-rode her, drawing her gaze to his as he parted the cluster of O'Neills and strode towards her, his eyes transmitting an unmistakable command that Hannah let things be.

Which threw her into more turmoil. She didn't want to let Tony down, but couldn't he see how much out of hand this could get if they kept feeding the misunderstanding?

''Hannah doesn't like to wear the ring when she's working—preparing food, cooking fish, wiping up, using her hands all the time,'' he explained.

All very reasonable. Hannah's heart was sinking at his persistence with the story. He was pinning her to it instead of...

''So I keep it in my pocket for her.''

All eyes turned to him as he pulled out a small jewellery box from his shorts pocket and held it out on the palm of his hand for every-one to see. It was like a conjuring trick.

Hannah couldn't believe it. Her parents moved aside to give him room to reach the galley counter directly in front of her and he placed the black velvet box on it—unmistakably a ring box. Even Hannah's eyes were glued to it now and it certainly wasn't disappearing in a puff of smoke.

"Give me your hand, Hannah."

She did. It seemed to her that her left hand lifted of its own accord. Tony opened the box, plucked out the ring, held her hand steady, and slid a fabulous emerald ring onto her third finger. The brilliant green gem winked up at her as if to say, "Here I am, as promised, all yours."

"Well, the cat's out of the bag now," Megan muttered smugly.

And it was! Everyone was oohing and aahing over the ring Tony had put on her hand, on her engagement finger, a very real, very serious ring that spoke more convincingly than any words could. If she tried to deny it…no, that option was gone. They would all think she was mad, treat her as mad, not realising that Tony had swept away her right to choose.

Her heart quivered at the sheer boldness of his move. He had to have ordered this ring for her, planned a proposal of marriage. How could he have made up his mind so fast?

Panic welled up in her.

It was too fast.

Much too fast.

"Take it back, Tony," More panic…did she really want him to? "Keep it for later," she hastily tagged on.

Later…when they were alone together…when this madhouse with her family was behind them…and she had time to think. All she knew now was she couldn't hand out a public rejection. The emerald ring was too serious. It forced her to look at what could be…*if* she truly was the only woman in the world for Tony King.

CHAPTER FOURTEEN

AT LAST they were in the jeep, driving away from the marina, away from her meddling family who had piled into a minibus for the trip back to their hotel, away from her fellow crew members and their happy grins exulting in how right they'd been about her and Tony.

Hannah didn't know what was right.

She simply felt intense relief that the barrage of well-meaning remarks and advice was over and she didn't have to smile anymore. Her face ached. Her head ached. And her heart ached, because it was torn between accepting the picture Tony had painted all day, and the fear there were too many flaws in it.

"Are you stressed out by your family...or by me, Hannah?" he asked quietly.

"Both," she answered on a heavy sigh.

He took one hand from the driving wheel and reached across to make physical contact with her, his fingers closing around her hand and gently squeezing. ''I didn't plan this, though I did intend to propose to you tonight.''

''I realise you were catapulted into it by my family thinking it was already a done deal, but...there was no deal between us, Tony, and...'' She shook her head, finding it difficult to articulate exactly how she felt about it.

''I pre-empted your choice.''

''Yes. Yes, you did.''

''Is that so bad, Hannah? Would you have chosen otherwise if we'd been alone together?''

''I don't know. You didn't give me the chance to think...to consider...to...to talk about it.''

''Then I guess we need to talk about it now.''

He squeezed her hand again before releasing it to bring the jeep to a halt outside her apartment. His calmness actually increased

Hannah's anxiety. She didn't hop out of the jeep when he did.

She sat staring at the big white wooden house that had been divided into four separate living quarters—not exactly flash apartments although they were completely private and she usually felt comfortable in hers. Her own space. Sharing it with Tony had been good, so why did she now feel he was invading it? Her heart was pounding so hard she couldn't think.

He opened the passenger door for her and still she didn't move, paralysed by a confusion she couldn't sort out. Wild doubts whirled through her mind as she stared at him. Was he Mr Right for her? Would he love her to her dying day and never look at another woman with desire? Was that an impossible dream?

Without a word, Tony stepped forward, scooped her off the passenger seat, and proceeded to carry her towards her front door, taking any decision out of her hands...again!

''Why are you doing this?'' It was more a plea than a protest. Her arms wound themselves around his neck and hung on, hardly a reaction that would deter him in his purpose.

"You look very fragile," he answered gruffly.

It was how she felt. And it was so easy to rest her head on his lovely broad shoulder and close her eyes and let the whole fraught day drift away, just breathe in his comforting maleness, feel his strong arms supporting her, the steady pumping of his heart within the warm wall of his chest.

He stood her on her feet to open the door to her apartment, but he was right behind her, his arms encircling her waist, his body like a protective shield she could lean against, his head bent to hers, his mouth softly grazing her ear.

"I'm sorry today was hard for you. I can't take it back, Hannah."

"I know," she murmured, unlocking the door, letting him in because she wanted him, needed him, and instinct was stronger than reason.

He closed the door and drew her into his embrace, face-to-face this time, and his eyes burned into hers as he spoke what had never been spoken between them. ''I love you, Hannah. You must know that, too.''

Her heart contracted. Why did those words hurt so much? They shouldn't hurt. They should be filling her with joy and happiness. Yet the shadows of pain and betrayal were flitting through her mind.

''Kiss me, Tony,'' she pleaded. ''Make me feel it.''

He kissed her with a fierce passion that flooded through her bloodstream and revitalised every cell in her body. It ignited a blaze of desire that obliterated shadows and the only thought pulsing through her mind was *yes, yes, yes.* She was so much *with him,* it was a jolt when he wrenched his mouth from hers and savagely muttered, ''No, no, no...this is wrong!''

''Why is it wrong?'' she asked, totally befuddled.

"You don't want to be stormed."

"Yes, I do."

"No…that's a quick fix. You want to feel loved. That's different."

He rained soft kisses around her face and took her mouth with a sensual tenderness that sent sweet shivers down her spine. He unbraided her hair and gently massaged her scalp as he kissed her some more, warmly, lovingly. It was so nice, relaxing, caring, Hannah basked in the pleasure of it, all her tensions melting away.

"I love the silkiness of your hair," he murmured, rubbing his cheek against it. "I love burying my face in it, breathing in its scent."

"I like smelling you, too," she whispered.

"And your breasts…" He started undressing her, stroking her clothes away, caressing her flesh as though it was a source of endless wonder. "You have beautiful breasts, Hannah. All of you is beautiful. I love looking at you, touching you…"

"I feel the same way about you. You're so completely perfect to me," she confessed, eagerly undressing him, wanting to see, to feel, and her heart was beating the refrain... Tony, Tony, Tony...

"Let me make love to you as I want to," he said, sweeping her off her feet again and carrying her to the bed. "Just lie here, Hannah, and feel me loving you."

It was always enthralling to her, being naked with him, the blissful intimacy of it, the freedom, revelling in his very masculine beauty, the innate power of his body. She never really thought of herself, except how lucky she was to have such a man as her lover.

Yet now, letting him do as he willed, focusing only on what he was doing to her, every erotic caress, every sensuous kiss, feeling her body responding—ripples of delight, quivers of excitement—it dawned on her that Tony *was* giving her the sense of every part of her being loved. More than loved...adored, cherished...and when he moved to give her the most intimate kiss of all, she was on fire to have him inside her, to show him how deeply she welcomed this loving, wishing it could go on forever.

It was utterly glorious when he finally surged into her. She embraced him with all she was—body, heart, mind, soul—and soared with him to one exquisite climax after another until they were both spent and lay tangled together in the sweet ecstasy of feeling completely fulfilled by each other.

''Marry me, Hannah,'' he murmured, pressing warm kisses over her hair. ''Nothing could feel more right than this.''

She sighed, wanting to agree with him. But it had only been a month. Maybe it was so wonderful because it was still new. ''Can't we wait awhile, Tony? Make sure it's going to last?'' she softly pleaded.

His chest rose and fell under her cheek and she sensed he was gathering himself to argue with her, yet when he spoke it was with a quiet calmness. "Why do you think it might not, Hannah?"

That was so hard to answer. How could she say she didn't trust him? That wasn't true. She did trust Tony. He had given her no reason not to trust him.

"Are you worried about the constancy of my feelings…or yours?" he asked when her silence had gone on too long.

"There…there hasn't been much time…to test them," she got out, struggling for words that wouldn't hurt.

"Hannah, I'm thirty-two years old. I've been with many women. Attractive women whom I've liked very much, whose company I've enjoyed. Not once in all that time, in all that experience, did I ever feel…this is the woman I want to share my life with. Until I met you. I can tell you unequivocally…that's not going to change for me."

Was it true? Could she believe it?

He gently rolled her onto her back and hitched himself up on his elbow to look down at her. Panic welled up in Hannah at the thought he was going to demand a decision from her. She was actually frightened to meet his gaze, knowing how compelling it could be. Yet his eyes were soft, kind, and a huge wave of grateful relief washed away the panic. He smiled, and her heart swelled with love for him.

''You knocked me out the day we met, Hannah O'Neill. And the very next time I saw you, the message started beating through my brain—this woman is mine. Since then, everything that's happened between us has confirmed that message, over and over again.''

He traced her lips with feather-light fingertips, reminding her of the tenderness he'd shown. ''Is it asking too much, wanting you to wear my ring? You can always hand it back to me if you decide I'm not the right man for you, Hannah.'' His smile turned into a tilted appeal. ''I can't force you to marry me, you know. That choice is very definitely yours.''

Tony...her husband...her partner for life...always loving her...the dream swam before her eyes, tantalisingly reachable...almost convincing...

''Let me put my ring back on your finger, as a promise from me. It doesn't lock you in. It simply says I love you and I want to marry you, and every time you look at it you can think about it.''

In a flash he was off the bed, fetching the ring box from his shorts pocket.

Hannah's mind was in a whirl. Was it all right to wear the ring, on the clear understanding she would hand it back if their relationship started feeling wrong, or less than what she felt was needed for a marriage to work? They were expected to have dinner with her family tonight. Everyone would expect to see it on her finger. If it wasn't...how was she to explain? But if it was there...they would expect more...and more...

Tony bounced back onto the bed, grabbed her left hand and slid the emerald onto her third finger. "Made for you," he declared triumphantly. "Fits perfectly."

It did. "How did you manage that?" she asked, staring down at the ring which was stirring a storm of turmoil. There were consequences if she fell in with Tony's plan. Much as she wanted to please him, make him happy with her, wearing this ring would start a train of events she wasn't ready to face.

"I waited until you fell asleep in my arms, then measured your finger," he answered, his tone rich with the pleasure he had taken in his forethought, pleasure she would take away if she refused to go along with him. "You didn't even stir," he went on. "Very peaceful sleep. Which just goes to show how good I am for you."

"You have been good for me, Tony," she acknowledged, and didn't want it to stop. But what if it did?

"And *will* be good for you."

His confident claim stirred the turmoil further. He'd chosen an emerald because Flynn had given her a diamond and Tony wanted to give her something different. But the words weren't different. Flynn had said he'd be good for her, too. It was too much to take on board right now. She couldn't do it.

A surge of desperate determination lifted her gaze to his. "If I wear this ring, everyone— my family, your family, all the people we know—will expect me to start planning our wedding." She shuddered from the sheer violence of feeling ripping through her. "I won't do it, Tony."

He frowned, his eyes probing hers with sharp intensity. "Do you mean…you don't want to wear my ring…or you don't want to get involved in planning a wedding?"

"They'll start it. They'll start it tonight. And you'll involve your grandmother tomorrow. They'll all look to me to do things…"

Her chest tightened at the mere thought of it. She could see Tony didn't understand. After all, wasn't it every woman's dream to plan her wedding? Except striving to produce that perfect day turned into an obsession, an obsession fed by the wedding merchants and the bride's family, claiming this had to be done and that had to be done if everything was to be *perfect*.

The groom was largely left out of it.

The bride was very busy.

So busy, the groom had time to look elsewhere, to start wondering if he'd made a mistake and some other woman might fill his needs better.

"I won't do it." She shook her head, feeling the whole destructive pressure of it and needing to break free of it, stay free of it. Her eyes begged understanding as she tried to explain. "It becomes an event that takes on a life of its own and it gobbles up too much. It...it consumes love instead of giving it room to grow strong and unbreakable. I'll get trapped into it because that's a bride's job. Not the groom's. And I won't be available when you want me..."

"You think I'll do what Flynn did."

His eyes accused her of misjudging him on totally unfair grounds.

"It's only been a month, Tony," she shot back at him, rebelling against his *certainty*. "You buy me a ring while everything's red-hot between us, when there's nothing getting in the way of doing whatever we like together…"

"You think it's going to cool?"

"I don't know. All I know is it has only been a month, and I will not be bull-dozed into planning a wedding that I end up having to cancel. I've been there, done that, and just the thought of it happening again freezes me up."

"What if it's still red-hot after six months, Hannah? Would you marry me then?"

She took a deep breath, trying to calm herself enough to consider. Six months. Any cracks in their relationship should be showing by then. If it was still the same, still as wonderful as it had been this past month… "Yes," she decided. "I'd feel more sure of everything being right for us if it lasted six months."

"Okay. On that basis, will you make a bargain with me?"

"What bargain?"

"You wear my ring, which you can give back at any time in the next five months if you don't feel right about us. At the end of that five months, if you're still wearing my ring, you will turn up as my bride at a wedding which I will arrange."

"You…arrange?"   Sheer   astonishment glazed her mind.

"I'll do all the planning, make all the arrangements. I'll buy what has to be bought, hire what has to be hired, book what has to be booked. All you'll need do is to turn up at the church at the specified time in the wedding dress which I'll supply. Five months from now."

She stared at him in amazement. "You'd take on all that…to marry me?"

He nodded, his eyes serious, absolute commitment written on his face. "I would like very much for us to have a wedding to remember, one we can look back on as a wonderful celebration of our marriage.''

Tears swam into her eyes. He was making it sound so real. And didn't it prove he loved her, being prepared to arrange a wedding himself? He wasn't even considering there was a risk in putting so much of himself on the line. Was he so sure they were right together?

''I want to give you that, Hannah,'' he said softly. ''But I do need something from you.''

Need...he had answered so many of her needs. The urge to give was instant and strong. She nodded for him to go on, too choked up to speak.

''Give me your word...there'll be no running away at the last minute.''

She swallowed hard and fervently replied, ''I wouldn't do that to you, Tony.'' Never would she deal out such painful humiliation...jilting him at the altar.

''Then...do we have a bargain?''

A shiver ran through her as she recalled Megan's words. *When the King family makes a commitment, it's rock-solid, providing you keep your side of the bargain.* Her eyes searched his as she asked, "Are you really sure about this, Tony?"

There was not so much as a flicker of uncertainty. "I'm sure," he said with a blaze of conviction that poured warmth into the cold places in her soul.

It felt good.

It was fair.

More than fair.

"Then yes. We have a bargain."

CHAPTER FIFTEEN

ISABELLA VALERI KING sat by the fountain in the loggia, waiting for Antonio to fly in from Innisfail. It was Friday, and on Sunday there would be a family luncheon here at the castle to celebrate his engagement to Hannah O'Neill, but he wanted this private meeting with her first.

His request had not surprised her. All was not as it should be. Isabella had reflected on the events of last weekend many times—the shock announcement on Saturday evening that the O'Neill family had arrived in Port Douglas—all twenty-four members—and he was going to marry Hannah. She was wearing his ring. No time to talk then. They were to dine with the O'Neill family and could he bring them all up to the castle for afternoon tea on Sunday?

Isabella had gone to bed that night filled with joy. Choosing Hannah O'Neill as the chef for *Duchess* had been the right move. Antonio had fallen in love with her—such a suitable young woman for him—and she would soon have a second grandson married.

She had enjoyed meeting the very large O'Neill family on Sunday—all of them so clever and talented—good stock—but she had felt uneasy at the way Antonio had been very protective of Hannah in front of them, fending off any questions directed at her about their future, answering them himself.

It was charmingly done. Isabella doubted the O'Neills had found anything amiss. When Antonio *performed,* he gave out so much dynamic energy, people didn't really notice anybody else and he had been in dazzling form that afternoon. No one seemed to notice that Hannah was being passive, letting him take control. No one except Isabella.

It didn't feel right to her. At the job interview, and on two subsequent meetings with her, Hannah had shown herself to be very active and enterprising, not at all backward in taking the initiative, confident in expressing herself—a delightful personality. Yet all that had been subdued on Sunday afternoon. Maybe she had wanted Antonio to shine in front of her family, but surely not as much as he had, even handling all the questions about wedding plans.

Tony had declared they would be married in Port Douglas—a decisive announcement with no input from Hannah, no excuse to her family why she did not choose to marry in Sydney from her parental home, which was the bride's prerogative. Oddly enough none of the O'Neills had protested this although Hannah's mother had looked sadly wistful for several moments before putting a cheerful face over her private feelings.

Antonio had gone on to state that the wedding ceremony would be held in the local church, *St. Mary's by the sea,* and the reception would be here at the castle. Then he had asked Isabella to show the older family members the ballroom while he and Hannah took the younger children up to the tower. Which was, perhaps, a reasonable arrangement, but why wouldn't Hannah want to check out the ballroom personally with her mother? This was not normal behaviour from a happy bride-to-be.

*Two years of running away…*that was what Antonio had said the night he had taken Hannah to Nautilis, intent on confronting the couple who had distressed her. Was she still *running away?* What did this mean in the context of consenting to marry Antonio?

The sound of the helicopter coming in broke into her disturbing thoughts.

Soon she would know the truth.

As much as she wanted Antonio married, it was so important to get it right. She remembered sitting here with Elizabeth whose three sons—the Kings of the Kimberley—had all made good marriages. Elizabeth had understood her need for the family to go on, building

on what had been built. She had also understood it couldn't be done without the right
women. Partners for life. Absolute commitment. No running away.

I have lived for eighty years, Isabella
thought, *years that have brought many joys
and many sorrows.* She wanted to see her
grandsons settled in good marriages with families of their own before she died...the last
achievement that would make sense of all the
rest. But time was getting shorter and shorter.
It went so fast now. Even so, it would be bad
if Antonio rushed into a marriage that was
wrong. Such a mistake would be very costly.

''Nonna...'' He emerged from the castle
foyer, closing one of the big entrance doors
behind him. ''...I thought you'd be inside.''

''I like sitting here, Antonio. I find
it...harmonious.''

It was eminently clear all was not harmo-
nious in his world. He brought tension with
him like an ill wind, as well as the battle en-

ergy that signalled a problem he was determined on facing and beating.

"I told Rosita not to bring us anything. I hope you don't mind," he said as he took the chair at the opposite end of the table to hers.

"You want to talk about Hannah without interruption," she surmised, her eyes informing him she was well aware of the sensitivity of this conversation. "I suspect you have moved too fast for her, Antonio."

A wry little smile acknowledged her perception. "One has to move fast to catch a butterfly, Nonna."

A butterfly? The fanciful allusion worried Isabella. A beautiful creature, yes, but... "It is wrong to pin one down," she pointed out, thinking such a fluttery characteristic was not what she had envisaged in a wife for Antonio.

"Hannah wants to fly with me. It's a matter of proving I won't stray from her side."

"You...stray?" Isabella shook her head, frowning over such a doubt. Hannah could not know him well enough. Once Antonio made up his mind, nothing could shift him from his course. "She needs more time with you."

"I've bought enough time," he claimed with confidence. "Hannah will wear my ring as long as it keeps feeling right. I've made a bargain with her and I need your help to carry it through, Nonna."

"Then you had best explain it to me."

He gave her the knowledge she was lacking, painting the backdrop to the current situation with all the shades she'd been missing. Hannah's previous high-pressure career as a top-line events organiser did not really surprise her. A useful talent to have in any walk of life, Isabella thought.

The story of her relationships with Flynn and Jodie Lovett was illuminating. That betrayal and the humiliation in front of her family explained much. It was relatively easy to piece together the problem. Hannah had suffered a massive loss of trust, not only in her own judgement of people, but also in planning for any future at all.

It took time to build trust, time to be convinced it would never be abused. Antonio had rushed in, knowing what his word was worth and expecting, as usual, to carry all before him, only to discover that winning his own way was not so simple.

Still, the bridal bargain he had made with Hannah was clever, possibly a masterstroke, though it laid him open to public humiliation should she cancel the wedding. He was taking all the risks, leaving Hannah free to walk away without any cost at all from their relationship.

The gift of love…

Did Hannah recognise it for what it was?

''So you see, Nonna, I need your help. You know how to go about planning a wedding. If you'll tell me what I have to do and when to do it…''

''Are you absolutely certain it will be right for both of you in the end, Antonio?'' she asked, not wanting to see him hurt.

''Nonna, I have never felt anything more right,'' he answered with quiet gravity. ''In my heart, I know Hannah loves me. And in her heart, she knows I love her. She is simply afraid to believe it.''

Was it true?

Or was it blind faith?

Five months…

Isabella gathered herself and stood up, knowing she had to trust Antonio's instincts. ''Come. We will go to the library so I can look up available dates for a wedding in my work diary. We must set a day. All planning begins with that.''

Antonio heaved a huge sigh of relief as he rose from his chair. A few quick steps and he was hugging her in an emotional overflow of gratitude. ''Thank you. I want the very best for Hannah, Nonna. It has to be the best.''

''The choices must be yours, Antonio. I will put them to you. I will see that your decisions are carried out. But this wedding must be your gift to Hannah, not mine. You do understand this?''

"Yes." He drew back to meet the challenge in her eyes with the fire in his soul. "I took the responsibility. I'll see it through. When Hannah walks down the aisle as my bride, Nonna, you'll see that it's right. She needs me to do this. It's the proof of my love for her."

A quest...that was what it was, and Hannah needed him to fulfil it.

Isabella smiled.

Getting his teeth into a quest was so Antonio. Did Hannah know instinctively it would bind him to her more effectively than anything else? She had agreed to the bargain. That alone had to mean she valued this relationship very highly. The butterfly might not yet be caught but it seemed she wanted to be caught. And to Antonio, failure was inconceivable.

Isabella hoped she would see Hannah O'Neill walk down the aisle to him as his bride. If she did...then it would be right.

CHAPTER SIXTEEN

THEY were all in the church…waiting. At least, all those who could fit into the small white church—the two families and the people closest to them—were jammed in…waiting.

The old wooden building, constructed in the traditional Queenslander style with its studs exposed on the outside, weatherboard cladding on the inside, was virtually a historic landmark in Port Douglas, positioned near the shoreline of Anzac Park, overlooking Dickenson Inlet. *St. Mary's by the sea* did not hold a big congregation. But outside, the whole park was filled with people…waiting.

Alex checked his watch.

Beside him, Matt muttered, ''She's running late.''

Tony's nerves tightened another notch.

''Only five minutes,'' Alex murmured.

But Hannah was always, always punctual. It must be someone else's fault, Tony fiercely reasoned. She wouldn't leave him standing here today. She'd promised. No running away at the last minute. His ring had still been on her finger yesterday. There was no need to worry.

He stared out the big picture window at the back of the church. It was a brilliant sunny afternoon yet there were no boats out on the inlet. No boats and no business being done in Port Douglas. Everything had stopped for *the wedding*.

It was like a festival day out there in the park. Marquees had been set up to serve food and drinks. Local bands were entertaining the crowd. An Aboriginal dance troupe had come down from Kuranda, adding their primitive colour to the celebratory atmosphere. People had flocked here from up and down the whole far north to witness the occasion. Even the ferals who shunned all society had left their shelters in the hills and come into town today.

Tony King was getting married.

If his bride turned up.

Did Hannah realise this was not like a city wedding where only those directly involved in it would be affected if it was cancelled? This was a community event and the King family always delivered what it promised. It wasn't just his pride at stake here. Almost a hundred years of tradition was riding on his judgement that Hannah loved him enough to be his bride.

His heart said she did.

His mind said she had to or there was no sense to what he felt with her.

His soul yearned for her to join him.

"Listen!" Alex nudged him, a huge grin breaking across his face. "She's on her way."

Cheers rising from the crowd outside. It had to mean they could see the horse-drawn buggies coming down Wharf Street from the Coral King Apartments where the O'Neill family had been housed for the wedding.

His grandmother and her great-grandson, Marco, would be in the first one, having come from the castle to head the procession. Alex's four-year-old son was to carry in the grey-velvet cushion on which lay the wedding rings. No doubt he was jiggling with excitement at being part of this grand occasion.

Alex's lovely wife, Gina, and Hannah's sister, Trish, would be riding in the second, wearing the emerald-green gowns he'd chosen for them.

Behind them would be Hannah with her father. Tony hoped she felt his love for her in everything she wore today—the bride of his choice. The wedding gown was relatively simple, a slim silky ankle-length dress which would hug her lovely curves, its low square-cut neckline and shoulder straps beaded with white pearls. Most meaningful of all to him was the headdress that would hold her veil.

Picard pearls—the best in the world from Broome at the coastal edge of the Kimberly. He'd contacted Jared King whom he'd met at Alex's wedding. The Kings of the Kimberly were descended from the same paternal line as his grandfather, and Jared ran the Picard Pearl Company.

His wife, Christabel, had requested photographs of Hannah and had created a special design for her from the ideas Tony had wanted expressed. It was his special gift to his bride on their wedding day. He hoped she loved it…was wearing it with love for him. She might not understand what it symbolised but he would tell her tonight—tonight when he made love to *his wife*.

Outside the noise of cheering and clapping increased. The jazz band broke into a joyous rendition of "When The Saints Come Marching In." The crowd started singing.

"What's the betting the band is leading the procession in?" Matt remarked, happy now that activity was in the air.

Everyone in the church started buzzing with anticipation. The waiting was almost over. Peter Owen handed his god-daughter, Alex's and Gina's new baby girl, to Rosita and moved to sit at the electronic keyboard, ready to play.

His white grand piano could not fit into this church, but it was waiting for him in the ballroom at the castle. For *this* wedding, he would do anything asked of him. Gina was to sing and he always accompanied Gina when she sang, joining in the duets with her.

The band's jazz playing stopped just outside the church. The crowd hushed. Tony took a deep breath to relax himself. In his mind's eye he could see the drivers of the buggies helping their passengers step down. A little shiver ran down his spine as the deep haunting throb of didgeridoos began.

The Aborigines who'd gathered were calling up the spirits of the dreamtime to wish this union well. It brought an eerie sense of ancient rites to this moment, reminding Tony that he belonged to this land which had proved fruitful for four generations of his family. The nature of it had to be respected and one had to work in harmony with it. That was the way of everything and the same had to be applied to marriage. Respect, harmony…

Silence.

Footsteps in the vestibule.

Alex and Matt, half turning to look.

Tony took another deep breath and followed suit. His grandmother was entering the church, walking up to the front pew. She was smiling at him. It was a smile that promised all was well.

Behind her he could see Marco and Gina and Trish lined up to make their entrance, but not Hannah as yet. No amount of sensible willpower could get rid of the butterflies in Tony's stomach. The moment his grandmother reached her place, Peter Owen started playing, the electronic keyboard producing quite a wonderful rendition of Mendelssohn's wedding march. There were speakers outside the church transmitting the ceremony to all who wanted to listen and the music seemed to swirl everywhere.

Marco started up the aisle, carefully carrying his cushion and grinning delightedly at his father who stood beside Tony, undoubtedly encouraging his little son. Gina came next. Then Trish. Tony forgot about breathing altogether when finally Hannah and her father moved into position to start their procession towards him.

His heart stopped.

She was here… Hannah…his bride…so radiantly beautiful…smiling at him…her green eyes sparkling…and holding the long white bridal veil was the plait of pearls, looping over the top of her head, each end fastened by exquisite gold and pearl butterflies, below them the long unplaited strands of pearls falling down beside her ears, mingling with the wavy tresses of her hair.

Two butterflies—one for him, one for her, joined by a bond that would intertwine them for the rest of their lives—and that was how it would be because she was here, willing to marry him, wanting to share the future with him, and she walked towards him, not one shadow of doubt dimming the happiness that shone from her and beamed straight into his heart, kick-starting it into a thunderous beat, a joyous drumming of love for this woman—*his* woman.

He held out his hand to her.

She took it.

The bargain was complete.

This was the time for them.

The link was unbreakable.

CHAPTER SEVENTEEN

DEAR Elizabeth,
It was a great pleasure to have you and your
family attending Antonio's and Hannah's
wedding. I feel very strongly that now we
have forged these ties which reach back to
the past, they must be carried into the future.
Heritage should be valued, not forgotten.
Which brings me to your very good advice
at the wedding.

You are right. I carry so many memories
with me that no one else has. And there are
the stories—almost legends now—of all my
father achieved from when he first landed in
this country. These things should be written
down so that future generations can read the
family history and know what has brought
them to where they are—perhaps even making them what they are as people. The genes

are passed on. I see the similarities in your sons and my grandsons. I think the King bloodline must be very strong. But then, so is my father's. It is a good mix.

I shall advertise for a person who is skilled in family research, someone who will know what questions to ask of the older members of the Italian community here, and who can assist me in organising all the accessible information. I must hunt up all the old photographs from the early days, although it is a shame they were always posed in a stiff fashion, not like those taken of Antonio and his bride.

I sit here, looking at a photograph of them taken on their wedding day, and it captures all the joy and love that shone from them. I remember the moment well. The photographer was trying to arrange some formal photographs by the fountain, but Antonio would have none of it.

"Take one of this!" he demanded and scooped Hannah off her feet. "Come fly with me!'' he said and whirled her around, her feet kicking through droplets of water, and they laughed at each other, so light-hearted and happy.

A wonderful photograph! I will enclose it with this letter. I'm sure it will bring a smile to your face. Although there is another one I like just as well. When Antonio set Hannah on her feet again, her arms were still around his neck and she looked up at him and said, ''I love you, Tony King.'' You cannot see the words but their faces show the depth of feeling between them. It is beautiful. I shall enclose it, too.

So my dear Elizabeth, another year has almost passed, but I am well satisfied with this one. Hannah told me she wants at least four children and I am sure Antonio will oblige her. Next year perhaps I will have another great-grandchild. I have much to look forward to.

Thank you again for your company at the wedding, and for your very good advice. I shall definitely proceed with recording a family history and it will be most interesting to see what eventuates from this worthwhile enterprise.

Perhaps I will have photographs of Matteo and his bride by the time it is ready for print. For me, it would make the story complete. I know you will understand this, Elizabeth. It is the women who give birth, who nurture families. I must find the right woman for Matteo. Then I can rest in peace.

With sincere respect and affection,
Isabella Valeri King

MILLS & BOON® PUBLISH EIGHT LARGE PRINT TITLES A MONTH. THESE ARE THE EIGHT TITLES FOR NOVEMBER 2002

❦

THE BRIDAL BARGAIN
Emma Darcy

THE TYCOON'S VIRGIN
Penny Jordan

TO MARRY McCLOUD
Carole Mortimer

MISTRESS OF LA RIOJA
Sharon Kendrick

STRATEGY FOR MARRIAGE
Margaret Way

THE TYCOON'S TAKEOVER
Liz Fielding

THE HONEYMOON PRIZE
Jessica Hart

HER FORBIDDEN BRIDEGROOM
Susan Fox

MILLS & BOON®

MILLS & BOON® PUBLISH EIGHT LARGE PRINT TITLES A MONTH. THESE ARE THE EIGHT TITLES FOR DECEMBER 2002

———————— ❧ ————————

THE HONEYMOON CONTRACT
Emma Darcy

ETHAN'S TEMPTRESS BRIDE
Michelle Reid

HIS CONVENIENT MARRIAGE
Sara Craven

THE ITALIAN'S TROPHY MISTRESS
Diana Hamilton

THE FIANCÉ FIX
Carole Mortimer

BRIDE BY DESIGN
Leigh Michaels

THE WHIRLWIND WEDDING
Day Leclaire

HER MARRIAGE SECRET
Darcy Maguire